Back from the Middle of Nowhere
By Uncle Fred Wilson

THE MIDDLE OF NOWHERE

CHAPTER I

"...and they won't know where I've gone."

Elizabeth Cotton

Sandy felt just a little bit uneasy about what he was doing—putting the whole inventory in storage. But he also felt uneasy about how little inventory there was. He had to make the decision alone since he hadn't been able to get hold of his brother Jake. It always seemed like Jake wound up making most of the decisions. Jake was older and was unmistakably a very good businessman. But they'd started the business together, and although Sandy felt a bit reluctant, Jake would expect him to use his best judgement when things didn't turn out as they'd planned. The plan had been that Sandy was going to stay in Virginia and keep the business going. Jake was heading out for the Far East on a buying trip. A trip they'd been putting off for a long time. Business hadn't been too good the last couple of years and they'd wound up spending too much of their income and watching their inventory dwindle. The original plan had been to wait until things picked up a bit and then go together. But that idea had to be scrapped. Jake would be in San Francisco staying with some old friends, Stan and Susan. He would be leaving on May 12 to fly to Singapore. If Sandy was able to get in touch with Jake, he would have to call Stan and Susan before then. Right out of nowhere, a well-dressed woman had come walking into the shop and offered to buy every Persian rug they had. Sandy offered her a price of $10,000- three quarters of retail- and she had accepted. That left Sandy with no rugs, two glass and bamboo dinette sets, 11 Turkish water pipes, 15 Afghani fleece coats, 16 hundred square feet of Malaysian woven floor mats, 22 glass Japanese net floats, $500 worth of semi-precious stone jewelry, and 300 or so brass and ceramic figurines. Without the Persian rugs, their main high-dollar item, the store would be showing very little business. On top of that, the $10,000 would be much better used in the Far East than in McClean Virginia.

1

The store's lease contract would be expiring the middle of May and the only point in keeping it would be if the store were to remain open, which, Sandy decided, was not worthwhile in the long run. The date was May 4th—Jake wasn't leaving until the 12th. Sandy called Stan and Susan. He let it ring about 12 times, then hung up. He thought maybe they were out for the evening buying groceries for the weekend. He would call back later. Jake would still be at their place now. Anyway, he wouldn't be leaving until the 12th.

Sandy looked at some storage places. They didn't have anything really big in the store, so he didn't need a lot of space. A space the size of a one-car garage was all he needed. He could give Barbara, their only employee, a temporary lay-off. She was used to it. Barbara was a plump, married woman, about 37 years old. They had hired her 6 years ago and she was still there. Not continuously- off and on- but most of the time. She thought of it as vacation, but it wasn't always planned for. They could have their phone line ring on her home phone, and she could take messages. He realized he was getting excited about traveling overseas. Things were getting messier politically all the time, but it was always exciting going to the East. Then, almost as much fun, was coming back and telling stories about it.

When Barbara came back from lunch, Sandy was sitting at the telephone desk staring at the floor. Barbara lit a cigarette. "You're cooking up something, aren't you," she said.

"Yes, I am, as a matter of fact."

"You're thinking about taking off and going with Jake?"

"You know me too well."

"Well, you know how the old saying goes."

"Yeah, we've still got the rugs and she still has the money."

"But… there's no big deal about going back to plan 'A', assuming the rugs get sold."

"I feel like it's a high probability. The thing I'm tossing around is… are you ready for this? Closing down Orient Express for a couple of months."

"But the lease runs out on the 15th."

"Right, so what I'm thinking: put the inventory in storage and let you keep the

2

business contacts going from your place. We were going to have to move sooner or later anyway, so why not at this point."

"Makes sense. But what will Jake think about it?"

"I don't know, I wish I could get hold of him. I've called about four times since yesterday morning and I'm not getting any answer."

"Well, you still have until Wednesday, at least."

"Yeah, but I want to leave by Tuesday. The garage called, Stan's car will be ready tomorrow. I'll drive it out to San Francisco."

"Things are really falling into place for you. You should be getting excited."

"Actually, I am. There are just two things: getting hold of Jake and getting the rugs sold."

"Not to mention driving to the West Coast."

"Oh, that's no problem, that's just a little drive in the country for me."

Stan and Susan's car was a four year old Plymouth station wagon built in the old dinosaur tradition. They had driven it to Virginia the previous fall in the midst of an inspiration to rediscover the backyard of America. An unexpected shake-up at Stan's place of employment had necessitated their quick return. They left the behemoth V-8 with Jake and Sandy. When Jake had started making plans to go to the Far East, he's had the old boat checked out, and found it to be in serious need of valve work. So Jake took it to Rudy, who did upholstery work but whose brother, Jesus, worked on Chrysler products. Jesus was thinking about moving back to New Mexico and needed the extra money. Anybody Rudy said was good, you could depend on. To Jesus it was just another old 318 with pitted valve seats and baked-on crud. You just get a six-pack, a wire brush and whatever else you need and go to town. Jesus had it all laced back up and would drop it off by Saturday morning.

Sandy and Barbara spent the rest of the day boxing up the store merchandise. A lot of it could stay in the display cases and the wicker baskets could be used to gather up the small novelty items. By late afternoon Sandy was already hauling loads with the van over to the storage place.

That evening, Sandy called Stan's place again. Still no answer. He wondered where they might be since they weren't home—especially when Jake was in town. He called long-distance information to make sure the number was correct. One thing he was sure of, Jake was leaving on the 12th. Sandy called the travel agency and booked himself on the same flight from San Francisco to Tokyo. Then all he had to do was be there early and find Jake before take-off time.

Jesus arrived at Sandy's place around 10 o'clock. The old Plymouth was humming like new. Sandy wanted to test drive it, so Jesus got in the passenger side. As they drove around the block Sandy listened to the engine and felt for the response when he stepped on the gas. It was running fine.

"Rudy tells me you're heading back to New Mexico."

"Yeah, the Chrysler dealer in Albuquerque has a couple guys retiring. I used to work in parts there and they want me to come back as assistant service manager."

"Will it pay pretty well?"

"Not really, but you can live a lot cheaper there, and there's a lot of little 'extras' in a job like that, so it won't be too bad. This place is so hurry, hurry, and there's so much crime, you know."

"Yeah, it's life in the big city."

Rudy was sitting in his car, waiting, when Sandy pulled up in front of the building. Jesus got into Rudy's car and they drove away. Sandy wondered what it would be like to have so many close relatives like Rudy. Jake was really the only family that Sandy had. Their parents had both died by the time they were teenagers. They then lived with a family friend 'Aunt Karen,' but she was no relation to them.

They'd been left an inheritance of around $10,000. Jake had started college as a fine arts major, but never graduated. He got started in the retail business by working in an antique store. He developed an interest in oriental art through his courses at the University of Maryland. In 1972, he and Sandy started the Orient Express. Sandy attended a total of three different schools. He finally got a B.S. in business administration from the Catholic University of America.

Neither of the two brothers ever married. They both had had a number of affairs, but none that lasted very long. Some people thought they were so

4

closely involved with each other that women felt like they were being left out and wound up becoming disillusioned; something about the fact that they shared an apartment and had a joint checking account made them seem impenetrable.

By Monday, everything was pretty well taken care of, with respect to the business. There were a few odds and ends that Sandy needed to talk to Barbara about. They had the shop evacuated by noon and a janitorial service was coming on Tuesday. The Persian rugs were loaded in the company van, which was parked at Barbara's place.

"Mrs. Wainscott will be calling tomorrow. Give her directions and then give me a call." Sandy told Barbara.

She nodded, then said, "Have you gotten through yet to Stan and Susan?"

"No, I really can't understand why."

"What are the possibilities they may be in San Francisco but just aren't there when you call?"

"Pretty unlikely, I'd say, but I can't seem to think of a better explanation, can you?"

"Something happened that made them want to remain unreachable."

"Yes. Can't imagine for what reason- but it could just be."

"Sandy, you might be walking in to something if you go out there."

"Well, for whatever reason, it couldn't have anything to do with Jake. And, besides, the only way we're going to find out is when I meet Jake at the airport."

"You mean, *if* you meet Jake at the airport."

"Oh, quit worrying. Everything has been going good. Don't put a damper on it now."

"Just use a little caution- please."

"Don't I always?" he grinned.

"Use a little more than usual."

Sandy spent the evening packing his clothes and other things he needed. He had cassettes of Willy Nelson and Dolly Parton, plus extra batteries for his tape player. He might get tired of listening to the somewhat compressed sound, but with Willy Nelson singing he could, somehow, endure the limitations. He knew well that once he was on his way, there would be things he wished he'd brought along, but he had to draw the line somewhere. He was looking for insect repellant when the phone rang.

"Hello."

"Hi, my name is Joe Stevens. Could I speak to Jake Rose?"

"Jake's not here right now. Could I take a message?"

"Oh, I'm trying to get hold of a friend, Stan Brown, who lives in San Francisco. I was told Jake might know how to get in touch with him."

"Stan Brown, let me think a minute, I'm trying to remember if I've heard that name." Sandy was trying to think, but not about Stan. "It does seem slightly familiar." Did this guy know he was lying? He couldn't decide. "Look, Jake should be calling me today or tomorrow. Can I have him call you?"

"No, don't bother. He'll be gone for quite a while then?"

"Yeah, couple of months. He's on a long vacation."

"I see. Well sorry to bother you."

"No bother at all Mr. Stevens. Sure I can't have Jake call you?"

"No, I've got some other people I can call. I'll call back if it's necessary. Thanks anyway."

"Sure. Bye now."

"Bye."

"You silver-tongued devil, you." Sandy thought. "Who in the hell was that and what did he want with Stan?" Sandy started to call Barbara, then changed his mind. He decided to wait until morning and give her a story that would keep her mind at ease.

He started adding things to his bag. Alcohol, acne cream, sun screen, pliers. The guy on the phone reminded him of an insurance salesman. Was he perhaps looking for Jake? But it tied in with Stan being out of touch. Also, he knew, if the guy was looking for Stan or Jake, he didn't know, at least, where one of them was. Anyway, if there was some trouble afoot, he had to get to California before he could be of any help.

He spent an hour picking out more tapes to take on the trip. Not so much for overseas, but for the long drive across the country. It could get quite boring, especially through Nebraska and Nevada. He finally decided on Chuck Mangione, Chick Corea, Dr. John, Asleep at the Wheel, Spyro Gyra, and Old and in the Way. He started watching TV, but soon realized he was losing his concentration. His mind kept switching back and forth, between talking to the Wainscott woman and weighing the possible answers to this non-communication with Jake. He got out a piece of paper and wrote everything down. He sketched a rough schedule for the rest of the week. Then he wrote down a list of possibilities concerning Stan, Jake, and the guy who'd said he was Joe Stevens. Then he made himself a Planter's Punch and sat down to watch the NBA Championship series. He hoped the Bullets could hang in there 'til the finals. After a while he felt a little looser.

The phone rang. It was 9:30. It was Barbara. "Mrs. Wainscott will be coming by in half an hour. How soon can you get here?"

"Do you have any coffee on?"

"Don't I always?"

"Then I'll be over as soon as I can get dressed."

Barbara and her husband and their two children lived on the ground floor of a four-plex of an old uptown neighborhood. It was a surprisingly comfortable place on the inside. On the outside it looked just old enough and nondescript enough to not be the target of burglars and con men.

Sandy arrived before Mrs. Wainscott and Barbara poured him some coffee. Barbara's three-year-old, Arthur, knelt on the chair across the table and watched Sandy intently.

"Why're you goin' oberseas Sanby?"

"Cause it's my duty."

"What's duty?"

"It's his job, Honey." said Barbara.

"What's my job?" Arthur asked.

"Your job is to help your Mommy." said Sandy

"Uh unh, she dudn't need any help."

"Sure she does, she needs to answer all your questions."

"I've been thinking," Barbara said, "With all the unrest in Iran, there may not be any goods available from there for a long time."

Mrs. Wainscott was a very handsome middle aged woman. Even with the crow's feet around her eyes and the lines around her mouth, she was striking. Her poise was practically impeccable. Sandy found himself glancing at her every so often, as if to convince himself she was real, and not some vision that he'd had. He felt as if he's known her for a very long time.

Stan's wagon was loaded and ready to go. He stopped at the bank. He deposited $1000 in the store's account so Barbara could cover expenses, and put the rest in traveler's checks. It was a perfect day. He left the car windows open just a crack and put on a tape. Willy was singing a song by Steve Fromholz.

"I'd have to be crazy, plumb out of my mind, to fall out of love with you."

The last time he'd seen Stan and Susan they'd talked at great length about what the West and Midwest were like. It was odd that they had seen so little of it in their lives. Sandy and Jake had traveled by car, up and down the East Coast many times. When they went to the West Coast, they flew. Besides stopovers in Denver, Chicago, or Omaha, they hadn't spent any time there at all.

On their recent trip, Stan and Susan had crossed the country avoiding the interstates as much as possible. Sandy didn't have the time to do that on this trip, but he promised himself one day he would.

There were a lot of clouds overhead, but in between the clouds, the sky in between them was a blue as it was in Carlo Ponti movies. There was a glitter of reflection off the streams and ponds as the old Plymouth rolled smoothly down the Pennsylvania turnpike for Pittsburgh. Willy Nelson was singing: "In the twilight glow I see them, blue eyes crying in the rainnnn..."

Sandy pulled into a truck stop and parked in front of the café. There were about a dozen people inside. One waitress, one fry cook, one busboy, a couple of truck drivers, and about six other people travelling together in a maroon and white VW van. The VW people were seated around a large round table. The oldest of them was grey haired and wearing a leather cowboy hat. They were eating breakfast and having a good time. They were kidding each other and each being kidded. Sandy decided that was the way to see the country- in a small amiable group. It would bring out the human values in inanimate

8

structure. Sandy ordered a cinnamon roll and a cup of coffee. The waitress brought it in a few seconds accompanied by a generous glob of butter. One of the women from the round table bunch walked over and sat down at Sandy's table. "Hi there," she said.

"Hi," he returned.

"My friends and I have a bet going that within our group, one of us has a connection with you in some tangible way. How'd you like to come sit with us for a moment so we can explore the possibilities?"

Sandy thought for a moment, "Sure, why not."

The guy in the cowboy hat was Bruce. The other five younger people were Sol, Denise, Larry, Rose, and Bill.

"I'm Sandy, pleased to meet you."

Bruce started out, "Ever been to Utah?"

"No,"

"Colorado?"

"Yeah, a few hours."

"Folklore Center?"

"No, museum."

"Hmm, how about Saratoga Springs New York?"

"No, can't say I have." Sandy started thinking of places he'd been and names of people. They traded questions for about fifteen minutes without success.

Bruce looked at Denise, "Looks like a loser this time." He looked back at Sandy. "What's your name again?"

"Sandy Rose."

"Aha, yelled Bruce." He jumped from his chair and pulled an object from his pocket. He set it on the table. It was a reddish-brown rock which looked like sandstone carved into a rose. "That there's a sand rose. And everyone knows Sand is short for Sandy."

In an instant the group were shouting at each other.

"Pay up. Pa-a-a-ay up!"

"No, no, no, no. No fair. It's not tangible."

"Sure it's tangible. It's hard as a rock."

Sandy groaned, "Sorry I started a controversy."

Finally they agreed the bet was off. It would be settled up later. They paid their check and went back outside. Sandy told them to look him up in D.C. sometime. They made the same offer about Saratoga Springs, New York.

Sandy headed on down the turnpike. Jerry Garcia was singing, "Gone are the days when the ladies said, please...gentle Jack Jones won't you come on to me. Brown eyed women and red grenadine... the bottle was dusty but the liquor was clean..."

If you look from the road at a ninety degree angle down the rows of corn, you see a long series of straight rows. If you look straight down those rows, you see a long series of parallel lines...one after another, after another. But you can only see down one row at a time. If it's hilly country, then you can have layouts like contour plowing, terracing and what-not. But in flat country, the straight parallel rows dominate the agricultural scene. Nearly everything around was green. The sky was a light blue with a few cumulus clouds.

Traffic on the interstate was light, one vehicle about every hundred yards. Sandy found it a pleasant contrast to the smog and congestion of the D. C. Beltway. The 55 mph speed limit took on a whole new meaning in the open country. He found he had to suppress the tendency to compete for position- to accelerate and brake in the quest for precious time. To suppress it he found he had to consciously emphasize a feeling of calmness, a relaxation that eventually proved to be enjoyable, once he got past the conscious control of it.

The car was like a sailboat- gliding along- floating on the wind. A light rain was falling as he drove into Omaha. This was heavy duty city. Miles, and miles, and miles of lights. He had been expecting the rest of the continent to be like Iowa, until this. Every damn thing was shiny with the wet glaze of the light drizzle. There were only the electric lights and the reflections thereof for miles in every direction.

The incredible flugelhorn was playing, "ta da da dunt dunt da da daaaa-a-ah; ta da da dunt dunt da da daaaa-a-ah." Mangione. Musicione. Whoosh, up to the door of the Best Western.

Sandy flopped down on the bed and turned on the TV. "Three out of four dentists recommend Trident sugarless gum for their patients who chew gum." Chunk, chunk "Cold air mass moving east will bring some precipitation..." Chunk, chunk... "Unseld, on the other hand, has remained very cool, slowing down the play and getting the ball inside, and really controlling the tempo of this ball game."

"Thank you, Bill. We'll be right back after this."

One pillow on top of another, shoes hit the floor; clunk, clunk. Washington was out in front thirteen points. He decided to watch the rest of the game, then, try to get some sleep. By the time the final buzzer sounded he was down for the count.

When he awoke the room was grey and he was surprised that it was already 8:30. The air felt damp and a little chilly as he walked to the Plymouth. He stuck the suitcase in the back and headed back for the interstate to try for another truck stop. The rain was falling in fine droplets; more like a heavy mist. The grass along the highway had an ethereal cast. It looked like it was very soft and yielding, like a pile carpet. The trees and bushes looked like they had been done by an impressionist painter. The green leaves had never been so vivid. There were no borders- only pure colors against a grey background.

The first truck stop he came to was gigantic. Not like the ones he had stopped in in Indiana and Iowa, where the waitress seemed to know everybody. But his stomach was growling and he sure needed some coffee. Before he got out of the car, he pulled on a sweater and congratulated himself on keeping it handy. He found an empty stool at the counter and the waitress was there in seconds.

"Coffee?"

"Yeah."

"Cream?"

"Please."

She filled his cup, then moved on down the counter with the coffee pot. He didn't pick up the menu. He knew she'd give him time if he did, and he knew what he wanted already.

"Whatcha gonna have, sweetie?"

"Two eggs over easy and patty sausage."

"Toast or biscuits?"

"Toast, no, make it biscuits."

The man on his right was carefully sliding his fried eggs in between his hotcakes. Then he spread butter over as much of the top as possible and drenched them in syrup. Sandy couldn't understand how a man could work up that much of an appetite sitting behind the wheel of a truck. But appetite, then, was a matter of personal taste.

Sandy didn't waste much time eating. The biscuits seemed like home-made and the coffee was fresh. After he's finished his second cup the waitress came by with the pot in her hand. He waved her away. No use getting strung out on coffee if all he had to do for the rest of the day was drive.

It was getting a little windy as he walked back outside. But it didn't seem as damp now with his stomach full of biscuits. He drove the car up beside the self-service pump and filled the tank with premium. The old boat could really suck down the gas- even on the highway. Things were going along smoothly. As he drove past Lincoln, Willie was singing, "Miracles appear in the strangest of places—fancy meeting you here. The last time I saw you was right out of Houston, sit down let me buy you a beer."

Sandy began to muse over the experiences of his past, when coincidences had brought people or things together unexpectedly. There was a typewriter he'd bought at an auction in New Jersey that, on the inside of the case, had the name and address of his of his fourth grade teacher. Then, there had been that incident when, sitting in a room full of strangers, someone mentioned a name- and it turned out to be the ex-spouse of one of the strangers. It's never called "just a coincidence"; it's always called "strange coincidence" or "unlikely coincidence", even though by definition, it is coincidence.

He stopped in Kearney and took a leak, then had another cup of coffee. He knew he wasn't running behind, but somehow, he had a nagging feeling that he had to push on. Maybe it was the coffee, or maybe it was just the anticipation of the trans-Pacific trip, but, he found it difficult to sit still. He felt like he had to keep moving. He had an overwhelming mind projection that he was having to absorb an astronomical amount of knowledge and experience in order to look at this amount of solid land the way it should be properly done. So just driving across it gave you no more than a few quick glances- all in only two dimensions. The third one was the clincher. Looking down these rows of corn as they drew away into infinity. The rolling hills were boundaries against the sky, but they afforded the most tangible effect of the enormousness of this country. The sky, itself, was gray and there was no distinct separation between it and the Earth. But the sky... there was so much of it. Some of it looked like boiling potato soup. Some of it looked like shaving cream. There were a few patches of blue. Not powder blue, like the East Coast, but a deep sapphire blue. Through these holes poured sunshine that made brightly lit spots that drifted across the hay-meadows and corn fields.

The drizzle had stopped. He wasn't exactly sure when. But the pavement looked dry- as if the area he'd driven into had missed getting rained on. There was still the wind. As he cruised along on the open stretches, he kept tugging to the right on the steering wheel to keep the big wagon in the lane. But when he pulled out around a big tractor-trailer rig, the car would suddenly lurch toward the truck as the wind was abruptly blocked by the big box trailer. He got used to the lurching, to some extent. When the wind comes only from one direction and is, more or less, steady, it becomes a motor-nerve automatic motion; like getting sea-legs on a boat. And this wind was steady and one-directional- right out of the north. The clouds that had looked turbulent before had amalgamated in the afternoon sky, which was now nearly solidly overcast. When sunset approached, visibility was becoming poor. The filtered sunlight left him color-blind and unable to distinguish details. Off to the north, the land was giving way to rolling hills. Sandy turned on the headlights and noticed immediately that tiny raindrops were striking the wind shield and were reflected in the headlight beams. Willy and Leon were singing, "...let me ride to the ridge where the west commences, gaze at the moon 'til I lose my senses, don't like hobbles and I can't stand fences, don't fence me in."

It wasn't long before Sandy noticed that the drizzle had become turbulent. The drops weren't accumulating on the windshield, but were bouncing off. Oh, no, how would Jake grab on to that? Snowing in western Nebraska in the middle of

May. Soon he noticed that the sky had become very low. When he looked up through the windshield, he could see only the swirling tiny snow crystals against a cold grey sky.

Abruptly, he ejected the tape and turned on the radio. He moved the dial from one end to the other, but he got only static. He remembered hearing that FM signals are good up to twenty miles. He switched to AM and very soon picked up a station in what sounded like "Carney." "...There are stockman's advisories out for the western two-thirds of the state, while in the North Platte and Ogallala areas, as much as fourteen inches of snow is predicted with blowing and drifting in some areas. So you folks out in that area, stay indoors, don't drive unless you absolutely have to, and if you do go out, be sure you have everything you need in case you have car trouble."

"Oh no," Sandy thought, "This sounds serious." What town was it that he just passed? North Platte. That's the town they'd mentioned on the radio. He decided to take the next exit. If there wasn't a motel there, he'd head back to North Platte- it couldn't be more than ten or fifteen miles. He drove on for several miles without coming to an exit. He was on the verge of turning across to the east bound lane when he saw the vague image of a highway sign illuminated by a lamp. A few seconds later he could make out the letters, "No Name exit, ¼ mile." He would see what No Name had to offer.

The exit ramp was blanketed with snow, so he slowed to about thirty mph and placed both hands firmly on the wheel as he headed up the incline. There was an electric sign visible through the blowing snow at the top of the ramp. When he got close enough to make it out, it said "No Name Laundromat, 50ct wash, 50ct dry." It was closed and dark. There were no other buildings. He figured he ought to head back to Johnny Carson's boyhood home. Looking north, he saw more lights, but the snow was so thick he couldn't make out what it was. He decided to take a few minutes to investigate before turning back. He drove for a mile and a half. The lights turned out to be yard lights around a metal building holding highway maintenance equipment. He pulled into the driveway to circle around in the parking area. The back tires spun as he made his loop and, as he headed back out, the car drifted to the right. He didn't quite make it to the highway. His right front tire went off the driveway into the ditch. The wagon jolted to a stop. The rear wheels were spinning.

Sandy threw it into reverse. The car inched backward and the wheels spun again, but he couldn't back it out. He got out to look at the tires. The blowing snow stung his face. He turned his back to it. The left rear tire was barely touching ground. He knew that the differential would keep that wheel spinning while the other one wouldn't. The whole side of his face and neck were aching from the icy blast.

He got back in the car and shut off the engine and the lights. He touched his face. It was numb from the cold. When he had stopped shivering, he rummaged through his bags and found a pullover sweater. He put it on and then put his light jacket over it. He had no gloves, no hat, and low shoes. Not even any whiskey. He couldn't believe it. Halfway across the country and stuck in a ditch in a snowstorm.

It was practically summer! Time for camping out- fishing. Why was it snowing? It couldn't be real. He lay back against the seat and took a long, deep breath. What would he do? It was Wednesday. Jake would be leaving Saturday afternoon. If they closed the highway it would be open again noon Thursday at the latest. If nothing else he could leave the car somewhere and fly to San Francisco. Stan could pick it up later. But then, he hadn't heard from Stan or Jake in the past week. He would have to talk to Barbara as soon as possible. He made a list of priorities. First, to get out of the ditch. He hoped the impact hadn't damaged the front end.

No, that wasn't the first priority. The first priority was to stay warm and dry until he got out of the ditch. In the meantime he had to stay calm. He turned the key to ACC and turned on the radio.

"Click. Poweee chuck, chuck…with the storm centered in eastern Wyoming and western Nebraska. Interstate 80 will be closed from North Platte, Nebraska to the Wyoming border. Stockman's advisories are out and only emergency traffic is moving in the western part of the state. Phone service is interrupted for about 70% of the area north of the interstate from North Platte westward. So, let me repeat this advisory, if you don't have to go out, stay indoors where it's warm and dry. We can expect the worst of it to be over by mid-afternoon tomorrow. Now back to you, Russ."

"Thanks, Howard, and now this word from Bristol-Myers...click."

Tomorrow afternoon! What would he do in the meantime? He felt a wave of despair- then a wave of anxiety. He felt confused. He realized that he would have to make an effort to keep calm and make rational choices until things got back to normal. It was just a snowstorm. He had to stay where he was until the weather cleared or until he was rescued. As soon as he could he'd call Barbara. It wasn't terribly cold in the car; a little below freezing, he figured. If he ran the engine he would have to make sure the exhaust pipe was clear. That would mean getting out of the car in that blowing snow. He decided against it.

He opened his suitcase and dumped it out. He made a pillow out of a pair of pants and some underwear; then he laid back on the front seat and pulled the clothes on top of him, spreading them out. There were a couple of newspapers on the floor. He pulled them apart, page by page, and crumpled them up to fill as much space as possible. When he finished, the whole space from the dashboard to the headrests, was filled with crumpled papers. He felt reasonably comfortable, so he laid his head back and tried to get some sleep.

He couldn't relax. There were too many uncertainties in his mind. What was happening with Jake, Stan, and Susan? Would he make it to San Francisco in time? Why was he driving across the country in the first place? All these questions hadn't seemed at all important as long as he was moving. Now that he was just sitting still, they kept circling in his mind like a buzzard around a crippled animal. There were no answers. He tried to conjure up something to reminisce about. A good story. A wedding. A funeral. Yes- Sanford L Rosenblum, found in a friend's car...now wait a minute! There's no need to get carried away. He thought about his childhood sweetheart. She had long hair, pale skin and green eyes. Like pure jade. Unforgettable. She turned out, as an adult, rather a quiet type at first. Then she moved away with the rest of her family and he never heard from her again. When they were eight years old, they'd decided to get married when they were big enough. He thought about it for a minute or two and decided that either he wasn't big enough to make a choice like that, or he never got big enough to do it.

Anyway, the image of those eyes always hung around in his mind, whenever anything was happening that had to do with eyes. He was leery of turning on the ignition and listening to the radio. The car might have a voltage leak which could run down the battery. He closed his eyes and started thinking about batiks and tapestries. He conjured up a vision of a large batik, all done in shades of brown with a monkey motif. Every time he opened his eyes, he saw swirling snowflakes in the glow of the yard lights. It was coming down almost horizontal. The thought of it hitting bare skin was enough to make him shudder. Pounding down in sheets, so it hit you broadside, was a chilling, galling prospect.

He couldn't sleep, he was too full of coffee. He was also hungry. He looked at his watch. It said 9:18. He felt rested, but anxious, He wished for some deep sleep, but it wouldn't come. The day's events were too thought-provoking. He lay there for what felt like hours, but when he checked his watch, not even an hour had gone by. The snow was coming down in sheets.

So this was the heartland of America. Vast and empty; though he found himself trapped. Trapped by the fury of nature, inside his man-made enclosure. He couldn't leave, but he couldn't stay. There was nothing to do but wait. He started to doze off. His mind wandered off along a country road and came to a deep river. He walked out onto a bridge and looked down. He turned and watched the river as it flowed away and away forever. Then he felt as though the river was standing still, while he and the bridge were rapidly moving backwards. He stood transfixed for several long minutes. Then he continued along the bridge. He walked and walked for hours, but still couldn't see the far bank. He looked back over his shoulder and couldn't see the bank from which he had come. He felt horribly alone and disoriented. The wind was blowing and his hair was flying around his head. His pants cuffs were whipping in the breeze and making a popping noise. The wind seemed to take his breath away so he had to suck in very hard to get enough air. The moon had appeared on the horizon and the popping noise was continuous.

He lifted his head and opened his eyes. In the dim light all he could see was the inside of the car. The windows were fogged over with moisture from his breath.

17

It took a few minutes for him to remember where he was and what had happened. The popping sound was like a Harley-Davidson.

Oh my god! Rescued by a biker. He reached in back of him to lower the window. When it was open a crack, a freezing blast stung his face. He quickly closed it.

"Over here!" he heard someone yell. He sat up and reached for the far window. As he rolled it down, a red-hooded and black-bearded face appeared. "Need some help?" the face asked.

"Yeah, I guess I do," Sandy replied. I'm Sandy Rose."

"I'm Bob Gage. Get yourself some wraps on and we'll go back to my place."

Sandy rummaged around for more clothes to put on. "How far is it?" he asked.

"About ten miles," said Bob. "Looks like you weren't prepared for a spring snowstorm."

"You're right, I haven't much to put on."

Bob stuck his head in the window and took a look around. "Pull a couple pair of them jockey shorts on over your head. Turn 'em sideways to each other to cover the holes. Get as many socks on your feet as you can. Forget the shoes, you won't be walking anyhow."

Sandy did as he was instructed. Soon he felt warm, though ridiculous.

"Now put a sock on each hand and we'll be ready to roll. Lean over my shoulder."

Bob was short, but burley, and he lifted Sandy's hundred and fifty pounds over his shoulder as easily as a sack of grain. The popping sound was coming from a big green tractor. Bob waded over to it and set Sandy down on the rear hitch.

"Now get both hands on the fender," Bob instructed, "and try not to fall off."

"I'll try," said Sandy.

Bob climbed into the seat and they were moving. It seemed to Sandy much like walking the deck of a moving boat. He kept his knees and elbows bent and felt for the give and take of the machine's motion.

"How'd you happen to come by here?" Sandy yelled.

"Had to come after my mail. From where my mailbox sits, I can see that equipment shed. I could see a bump in the snow and I thought it might be a car.

18

I was right." Bob yelled back.

"I'm glad you went after your mail. Were you expecting something important?"

"Yeah, bull semen. It comes frozen on dry ice. If it thaws out, it's useless."

"Was it thawed out?"

"I doubt it."

Sandy's face was being stung by the icy blast and was beginning to ache, but it didn't seem to matter as much, now that he knew he would be getting warm again in ten miles. But god! It seemed like they were barely crawling. Dozens of questions raced through his brain; mainly related to where certain people were and what they were doing. It all seemed to be in another world, which, in a way, it was. The only people he knew about for sure were himself and this Good Samaritan named Bob Gage. What kind of man was this who had to travel ten miles to his mailbox and who brought strangers home on the back of his tractor? Was he a devoutly religious man, or a rowdy redneck who drank whiskey out of long neck bottles? Was he open-minded or a bigot? Sandy thought maybe he'd better not mention his being of Jewish descent until he found out more about the man. The mailbox read R. Gage and L. Denton. After they'd passed that point, the road was anything but straight. It twisted and undulated so much that he had a hard time keeping his balance. He had to take turns standing on one foot, then the other to keep the balls of his feet from getting numb.

"How long do you think it will keep snowing?" he yelled.

"It's almost quit now."

"You mean this is mostly what the wind's blowing around?"

"Yep, blowing and drifting."

"I don't know if I'm glad to hear that or not."

"Yeah, give thanks for small favors."

Small favors, indeed. What difference is a favor when your life is at stake? So small, yet so big. So easy, yet so important.

Bob yelled back, "How do you like it here so far?"

Sandy broke into laughter. He couldn't stop for several minutes. Bob was laughing too. Finally he caught his breath.

"Owooo...I love it!" They both erupted again into laughter. Tears were streaming down Sandy's face and he was giggling uncontrollably. He didn't feel so cold then.

They were within a hundred feet of the house before Sandy could make out the shape of it. It was a two story white frame building, much like most of the farm houses in the Midwest. Smoke was rising from the chimney. Snow was piled up deeply along one side, the ground was nearly bare. The windows were covered with polyethylene sheets.

Bob pulled up next to the lee side of the house and dismounted. Sandy hopped down and walked to the doorway. He felt warmer immediately. Bob was retrieving his treasured bull semen from his tool box. "Go on in."

Sandy was about to say, "You mean it's not locked?" then it occurred to him what a silly question it was. He went in with Bob close at his heels. It felt like heaven. A warm house with the snow and wind sealed out. It was like it had been in DC in mid-December, when he'd had to take a cab home late at night. But this was Nebraska- the heartland. What the hell did it look like, besides the fact it was hilly?

Bob handed Sandy a blanket and broke out laughing. Sandy put a hand on his head, then he was laughing too. As he removed the jockey shorts from around his ears, he heaved a sigh of relief, wrapping the blanket around his shoulders and sinking into the nearest chair. Bob handed him a jelly glass with an inch of whiskey in the bottom. It went down like a warm breeze blowing across his frozen face. Bob was tossing hunks of two-by-fours into the round black cast-iron stove. Then he, too, sat down and started pulling off his rubber boots and several pairs of socks.

"If you get sleepy, just flop down over there on the sofa. Feed a chunk or two of wood into the stove every now and then, and we'll have a warm house through the rest of this storm. I'll have to go back out- we're calving, and this weather ain't helping one bit. My sister will most likely be in after a while."

"You're doing what?"

"Calves being born- and we're losing them right and left. Trying to get in as many as we can, but, we're running out of space in the barn."

"Holy shit!"

"My feelings exactly. A hell of a note. So make yourself comfortable. Stay warm…" Sandy was already falling asleep. Two minutes went by and Bob started pulling his socks and boots back on. Once he had his rubber boots on, he stood and pulled on his hooded sweater and parka. He put on his heavy mittens and slapped his hands together in anticipation of the feel of solid metal and the wetness of the blinding snow. He stood for a moment or two with clenched fists and squinted eyes, then stepped into the lean-to, then stepped outside and slammed the outside door. He mounted his tractor, pulled out the throttle and rolled off into the blizzard. During the course of the night he brought in sixteen baby calves- worth potentially a thousand dollars each if he kept them alive for a year. He'd leave them inside for a few hours to get nice and dry and warm, then they could manage to make it alongside their mothers for the next year or so.

Whenever he came across a calf less than a day old, he carried it across his lap on the tractor while its mother tagged along behind. Sometimes he carried two at once to save time. Sometimes one would be so weak and in shock that it was a waste of time. Bob's sister, Louise, was also out bringing calves in, but she was on horseback.

The area to the north of the house had steeper hills and was deeply drifted in places. They had a few good cow horses which were tough and healthy, but a horse would be good for only five or six trips out and back. The drifts and the slopes were too exhausting. From out there she heard Bob come in and leave again, and rode in shortly thereafter. She was riding Old Copper. He stood sixteen hands, and had big feet and a big head. He was very strong. She poured him a quart of sweet feed and hung the bridle around his neck, leaving him in the barn before she headed for the house.

She was mildly surprised to find a stranger lying on the couch. She doubted if he was there for a social call. She had the weather-beaten appearance of a western country girl. In New York they would take her for thirty-five or more- but she was twenty-eight. She weighed about a hundred and forty at five feet five inches but she could throw seventy pound bales of alfalfa onto a haystack four feet above her head. She had blue eyes and dark blond hair. There was a horizontal scar across her left cheek.

She poured herself some coffee and then sat down and pulled off her boots. She figured she'd make about two more trips out on Copper, then switch to Ferdinand. Ferd was getting a little slow in his old age, but he didn't seem to mind the weather.

She studied Sandy's face for a few minutes and decided that he looked honest. That didn't necessarily mean he was, but he looked that way. "Well sleep tight, dude, while you can, as soon as this storm blows over, this girl is going to sleep twenty-four hours and then take a nap."

It was daylight when Sandy opened his eyes. At first he thought he was still in the front of the Plymouth. Then, bit by bit, it all replayed in his head. This was... Bob and Louise's place, somewhere...no...No Name, Nebraska. He couldn't tell if it was still snowing, but it was still overcast. He looked at his watch. It said 10:00 AM. But that was Eastern time. It had to be 8:00 AM here. There was a humming sound coming from outdoors. Humming interspersed with "waaah". He couldn't see out of the windows, they were covered with plastic wrap- but it had to be cattle. Sandy had just pulled his pants on when he heard stomping outside the door. Louise came in.

"Well, you're up! I'm Louise, you must be Sandy."

"Good morning." Sandy said, "How are things going?"

"We lost a few. But I think we made out as well as could be expected. Say, I'll make you a deal. I'll make us some breakfast if you'll go out and help Bob throw out some hay bales."

"Sure, I'll be glad to, but I didn't come too well prepared..."

"No problem, you can probably get into these Carharts," Louise told him, "and I'm sure we can find you some gloves."

"What about my feet? I'm about an eight and a half."

"I think there's some high-top rubber boots that we use for shoveling manure."

Sandy rummaged through a drawer which was filled with a variety of gloves and mittens. Most had no match. He found a rubber coated one for his left hand and a leather palmed ski mitten for his right.

"Try these on." Louise handed him some black rubber boots with red soles. Sandy had three pairs of socks on, and the boots fit perfectly.

Sandy said, "Well, I'd better get out there before I start sweating. See you later."

"Morning, Mr. Rose. I guess Sis talked you into taking over." Bob tossed a bale onto the pile. Sandy grabbed a bale by the twine. He pulled it up to waist level and managed to swing it up and onto the wagon.

"She said she'd make breakfast."

Bob grinned, "Either that or she's asleep already. Let's get about ten more on, then we'll roll."

When they had the hay loaded, Bob climbed onto the D-6 Caterpillar. "You ride back there. As soon as we get about a quarter mile off, start throwing them off. About every fifty feet or so. Try to fling it so you pull the yarn off and it busts open." Sandy signaled OK.

The cattle that crowded in around the barn and house followed them out toward the hills. Sandy soon developed the technique of dropping a bale off the back while holding onto the twine so that the hay fanned out and easily fell apart as the cows nosed into it hungrily. At first the animals crowded around the first few bales, but eventually most of them tagged along until they were all strung out along the road. When it was all unloaded, Bob pulled up and let the Cat idle.

"So, what do you do, Sandy?"

"My brother and I are in the oriental import business. We have a store in the Washington, DC area. I was on my way to meet my brother, Jake, in Frisco. We were going to fly overseas on a buying trip. Well, it's a long story, but I was supposed to be there tomorrow morning."

"And here you are in the middle of nowhere. Well you and Jake are delayed a day or two, but you're safe and sound."

"Yeah, safe and sound. But it's not quite that simple." Bob was unhitching the wagon. Sandy stood by while Bob turned the Cat around. Then climbed up in back of the seat as they headed back towards the house.

"Why isn't it that simple?" Bob asked loud enough to be heard over the diesel clatter.

You see, Jake doesn't know I'm coming. So if he doesn't hear from me, he'll just leave anyway."

"Well, maybe the phone line will be working again soon and you can call him."

"Yeah….well, all I can do is page him at the airport. There's nowhere I can reach him before that."

"Huh? This story is getting to be more complicated all the time."

"Yes…it is. Too complex to be true, in fact."

"Well, tell me about it back at the house, I'm getting hoarse."

Most of the cows raised their heads as the Cat crawled by. They seemed to be staring, waiting for some signal, but they kept on chewing, with big wisps of hay in their mouths. Sandy mulled over what they would be eating for breakfast. Maybe eggs…pancakes, or oatmeal. Anything sounded good at the moment. He was thirsty, mostly, but he hadn't eaten since the day before.

The sun was breaking through the clouds now, but there was an intermittent gusty breeze. Bob pulled the Cat up on the lee side of the barn and shut it off. The silence felt sudden and sharp. There was the distant sound of the cattle occasionally interspersed with that overwhelming silence. There were pleasant aromas coming from the kitchen as Bob and Sandy approached the door.

Steaks were grilling on the top of the stove and Louise was spreading butter on a stack of toast.

She looked at Sandy. "If you want coffee, I guess you'll have to make it yourself. I don't think Bob's in the mood for it right now."

Bob grinned, "No way, just want to eat and sleep. Louise, is the phone working yet?"

"Nope, dead as a door nail. Sorry, Sandy, looks like we're stranded and incommunicado for the time being. How do you like your steak?"

"Uh, medium. No, it's ok, last night I more or less resigned myself to the fact that I wouldn't make it to San Francisco in time…maybe coffee wouldn't be such a good idea anyway."

The steaks sizzled as Louise gently lifted each one up and over on the grill. "So what other choices do you have left?"

24

"Well, I've still got to get this car back to its owner in California. I don't know where my brother is, but our secretary in DC can be reached by Jake or me at any time. We've both got money on hand to invest. So I'll just go back and reopen the store... and hope I hear from Jake soon."

Louise said, "It sounds like you don't have too many choices."

"You're right about that. The fact is, though, that I guess I've been guilty of not staying in touch too often, myself. So now it comes back on me. Our Girl Friday might know exactly what's going on with the West Coast Crowd, but she's so used to my lack of communication, she won't give it a thought."

Bob laughed, "Well... if you were looking for a lack of communication, I'd say you found it."

"I can hardly believe it..." Sandy's voice trailed off.

Bob was filling a glass with ice. "What are you drinking, Sis?"

"Red Zinger. Sandy?"

"I think I'll stay with water."

Bob filled a quart jar with ice cubes, filled it with water and set it in front of Sandy. Sandy smiled. "I can drink this, I guess?"

"Hell yes you can drink it. What else would you do with it?"

"Oh, I believe you, it's just that you'd be amazed at how many places in the world you can't drink the water."

Louise set the plates down on the table and they all dug in. It was several minutes before anyone spoke.

"What kind of steaks are these?" Sandy asked.

"Rib eye," Bob said from the corner of his mouth.

"It's the best I've ever tasted," Sandy commented, "I don't think I've ever had one before."

"Restaurants," Louise said, "are all fillet crazy. They think the front end of a cow isn't good for anything."

"It's the fat layered in with the meat," Bob added, "that makes it so tasty."

"This message from your Nebraska Beef Growers Association," Louise mocked.

Sandy started chuckling. He put his right fingertips on his forehead. "You know, I just realized, this is what you people do."

"Yeah." Bob drawled. "You might say this is what we do. The best part about it is that when most people put in an eight hour day, we're putting in a twelve hour day, and even then, it could be longer."

"Why is that the best part?"

"Well if you're so busy and so tired, you don't have the time and energy to get in trouble."

"Yeah, I could see that," Sandy said, "forgive me if I'm sounding naïve, but it just seems unusual that you can eat what you produce. That seems like it would be an enviable position to most people."

"Like everything else," Bob responded, "it has its drawbacks. But what about this mission you're on?"

Sandy started by telling them about Jake and the business, then worked his way back to the rugs, the station wagon, and the rest of the inventory. By 2:00 PM Bob and Louise were nodding off. He stood in the kitchen window and looked out. The snow was very uneven. As if the ocean, on a windy day were frozen instantly and sprinkled with powdered sugar. He contemplated the ten miles back to the car. He shut his eyes. Better not to think about not moving. But how to relax? He ran some water into the sink and started washing the dishes. Louise staggered to the couch. Bob was already stretched out in front of the stove. The dishes clean, Sandy saw no reason to try to do anything at the moment. He grabbed a magazine from below the telephone and began reading. He flopped down in a beanbag under a lamp. "A New Method for Dealing with Your Bot Problem." In twenty minutes he could no longer keep his eyes open and he dozed off. He had a dream about hiding in the forest from his brother Jake. They had to stay quiet so the Treasury Agents wouldn't find them, but they were surrounded by giant bot flies hovering close by- trying to lay eggs on their clothing. Finally they had to make a run for it, guns or not, they were taking their chances with the G-men rather than staying with the bot flies. When the G-men saw them coming, they turned and fled across the pasture with the bot flies in hot pursuit. He was awakened by the telephone ringing.

"Hello."

"Is this XA5-0701?" Sandy looked at the phone.

"Yes it is."

"Your phone is in working order, Sir."

"Thank you, operator."

"Surely, good-bye."

Sandy couldn't think of anyone else to call, so he called Barbara.

"Orient Express Imported Gifts."

"Barbara, this is Sandy. What's going on?"

"You tell me first."

"I'm stranded, out in the middle of nowhere, and it'll be at least…oh, about six hours before I can get out of here."

"Don't worry about catching up with your brother, he's already gone."

"Already gone?"

"Yeah, left last night."

"But why?"

"Seems these Italian people think Stan murdered their uncle with a tire iron. He did get into an argument with the man, but it was somebody else who killed him later."

"So Stan and Susan have gone into hiding?"

"That's about the size of it; until the problem gets resolved."

"Oh, God, that's grim. So what has Jake got to do with it?"

"Jake rented a car at the airport. They knew he was a friend of Stan's and got the name and address from the car rental office."

"This sounds like the work of experienced criminals."

"I think so too."

"Here's what we'll do. If you hear from Stan, just tell him I'm somewhere in Nebraska. I'll be keeping you posted on what's happening with me and you can be liaison for us."

"Where in Nebraska?"

"It's a place called 'No Name'."

"Sandy, are you sober?"

"Not exactly, but it's no bull-shit… except in a way…no, really I'm fine. Everything is all right. It'll just be a few hours before I can leave here. So don't fret about me. Just keep me posted. Here's the number…" Their conversation over, Sandy hung up the phone. All of a sudden he had a feeling of calmness come over him. He flopped down in the beanbag again. This time when he dozed off, he didn't dream.

Sandy woke up at about 5:00 PM. His hosts were still sleeping. The sound of dripping water was all around. He put the rubber boots on and went outside. There was a breeze blowing from the direction of the sun. Not a warm breeze, but a pleasant one. Water was dripping from the roof of the house. There were dark patches on the ground where the snow had melted. The sky was spectacular. There were high ribbons of clouds, mostly dark, but sprinkled here and there with sunlight. He was watching the clouds on the horizon when suddenly a rainbow appeared; more than a half circle, clear and bright. Looking directly up, Sandy could see the faintest of the sunlit clouds with pure, deep blue beyond. There was no haze, no mist, no dust or smoke. Just the rolling hills, the sky full of clouds, and the awe-inspiring rainbow. He stood in one spot for several minutes, just looking and breathing. He didn't hear the footsteps until Louise was about ten feet away.

"Whatcha doin', Sandy?"

"Just feeling. Standing and feeling."

"Is that a tear I detect in your eye?"

"Yeah…, I guess."

"Not sad, are you?"

"No, no, not at all. In fact, I'm quite happy."

"Just sentimental? I'm that way myself, I guess."

"Well, from one sentimental fool to another, this is about the most fantastic fireworks show I've ever seen."

"What about the chinook?" Sandy looked puzzled. "The chinook. The warm breeze that's blowing. It's a harbinger of spring"

"Oh, I guess I've heard of that before. Yeah, that's beautiful too."

"But there's one thing missing," Louise went on, "what you need is the touch of another sentimental fool."

She slipped her left arm around Sandy's waist. He smiled and slid his right arm around her shoulders. She squeezed the side of his waist with her hand and fingers. It was a warm, friendly squeeze. Not soft and titillating like a passive woman's, but firm and reassuring like a mother or a grandmother. But it was an arousing squeeze as well.

Sandy pulled her against his chest and hugged her closely. She laid her head across his shoulder and hugged back. He had never been hugged like that by a woman. It was firm- like a good handshake. Not just an embrace, but a squeeze.

"I've got some coffee going, if you want some." she said.

"Sounds all right." They walked back to the house, side by side. Bob was sitting at the kitchen table watching the news on TV. As Sandy and Louise walked in, he got up and poured them each a cup of coffee. There was a brief story about the Shah of Iran as the rebellion against him grew more open and vocal. When the sports news came on, Bob looked over at Sandy.

"Let's figure on pulling that car out first thing tomorrow, if that's ok." Bob glanced over at his sister.

"Oh, there's no real rush, now that I'm going home anyway, but you don't have to bother, I'll just call a wrecker." Sandy explained.

Louise laughed, "You wouldn't be saying that if you knew how much it costs to get a wrecker out here."

Bob added, "Aw, no problem, you've helped us and haven't been any trouble."

"Well, ok, I guess you talked me into it."

"Can you ride a horse?" Louise asked.

"Oh...yeah, to some extent."

"We're planning to go have a look around in just a bit. You're welcome to come along, if you'd like to," Bob offered.

Sandy couldn't conceal his smile. "Yeah, sure."

"Well, ok," said Bob. "I've got just the horse for you, ol' Ferdinand." Then they talked about their respective families. Louise noted that both their families had two children and that none of their parents were living. Sandy pointed out that he and his brother were very close, just as Bob and Louise were. Maybe it was related to the fact that the only family they had was each other.

Bob called up the horses from the pasture and into the corral. They filed in and went straight for their grain rations, which Louise had doled out into the trough. Bob went in and slipped a rope halter on each one chosen for the ride. The other horses moved aside as they saddled up.

Ol' Ferd was a strawberry roan. Louise's mount was Baldy- an old bay gelding. Bob had Ladybug, a young palomino mare. Sandy could barely contain his excitement as he watched Louise handling the gear and tried to match her motions. She said, "Thing to remember is *tell* him what you want him to do, then wait for him to respond. It's not like a car where you hit the brakes and it stops. You give him the message- wait for him to do it before you give him another signal. Basically he'll follow Bob and me until we get down to business."

Heading out into the hills, Sandy couldn't quite believe it was real. Heading out to doctor some cows. They spotted several calves that were down, but as they approached their mothers nudged them to their feet and they scampered off. They found a few, though, that looked weak and shaky. With these, Louise and Sandy kept the cows occupied while Bob gave the calves a shot of mixed vaccines and an antibiotic shot.

In the gathering darkness, they had to start working by flashlight, but they kept at it as long as they could. Sandy soon discovered that he could lay the reins down on the old roan's neck and he would stand calmly while Sandy aimed the flashlight where it was needed. They finally quit when it was pitch dark and impossible to continue. Heading back, the horses broke into a trot without encouragement.

"Sandy, if he breaks into a lope, check him with a quick jerk, then let up," Bob said.

When they arrived at the barn, Sandy felt a little disappointed that it was time to quit.

"It's just a damn shame," Bob grumbled, "that we can't do things the way we should."

"Bob, we did the best we could," Louise said softly.

"I know, Sis, it's just a cryin' shame. We're losing God knows how many just because we can't get the job done."

Louise led their three mounts into the corral and doled out some grain for each,

30

giving each horse a brisk rubdown. As they headed for the house, Sandy thought about the millions of street kids back in DC and all over the country, who would give anything to get to do what he had just done. "Bob, forgive me for asking a dumb question, but isn't there a way to get more help?" Sandy asked.

"No, it's not a dumb question. It's a question I keep asking myself all the time. I can borrow money. I can buy equipment. I can sell stock. I can do every damn thing I need to do. But I can't keep employees. I can feed and house them, but I can't pay them enough to keep them here. This country runs on beef. MacDonald's has sold so many millions of hamburgers they've lost count. But a man can't make a living raising cattle unless he's worth over two million dollars."

Sandy didn't quite know what to say, so he just nodded his head.

That night over supper, they talked about their families. Bob had been married and divorced; Sandy had had a live-in relationship that went sour when she tried to keep Jake out of his life. Louise had been married for two years when her husband died in an accident. It had been three years since then, but she still had a hard time accepting it in her mind.

"I still feel like he could come walking in that door right now."

Bob's wife thought it would be romantic to live in western Nebraska on a cattle ranch. What she failed to realize was how hard you had to work, and how little you had to get by on. She'd stayed a little over a year. Before she left, Bob asked her if she thought he'd broken faith with her. She never answered him. That was what bothered him the most. He felt like he's been robbed of emotions and never got an "I'm sorry I did this to you." for it. Sandy was a bit surprised to find out that Bob wrote poetry. It seemed so out of character for such a burly man. He promised to let Sandy read through some of it before he left.

The time was approaching eleven when Bob stood up and announced he was turning in. Sandy and Louise sat there for several minutes in silence. Finally, Louise put her hand on Sandy's shoulder. He looked at her and she looked back. Sandy couldn't think of anything else to do, so he kissed her. It was a kiss that lasted a long time. When it was over, they held each other with their hands on each other's shoulders. A long minute passed. Louise took a long breath.

"Want to?"

"Sure."

Louise giggled. "You're supposed to say, 'Want to what?' Arm wrestle? No, just kidding. Want to sleep together?"

"Same answer. But it'll have to be your place since mine is so far away."

"It's a deal."

They went to the guest bedroom, mainly because it was close by. Neither of them had much to say. It seemed as though it wasn't necessary. Sandy felt different than he ever had before with a woman. She didn't wait to be touched. She gave and took actively, not dominantly, but not passively. Her kisses were firm and responsive. Her hands felt deliberate and self-assured.

After they made love they stayed cuddled together for a long time. He raised up on his elbows as they nibbled at each other's lips. With her fingertips she stroked his sides from armpits to buttocks and back. Slowly he felt himself swelling again. He knew she hadn't climaxed, so he asked her if she'd like to start again. She replied by smiling and wrapping her legs around his lower back. Within a few minutes she began to climax and he reached his second one. They fell asleep in each other's arms.

Morning came early. The sun was barely up when they ate breakfast. Bob went off to do chores, while Louise and Sandy went off to rescue the Plymouth. They rode down on the tractor to the equipment shed. The right front wheel wasn't touching ground. It dangled over the edge of the culvert. Sandy climbed onto the front bumper and raised the hood. The radiator was pushed back into the fan on the right side. Louise stuck her head under the hood. She reached across to grasp the top of the radiator.

"Strap's broken."

"Yeah, lucky I didn't start the engine."

"Hold on, I'll get some wire." Louise walked back to the tractor and unwound a piece of baling wire from the rear hitch. "This'll hold it 'til we get it up the hill."

Sandy lay on his back and wrapped the tow chain around the bumper mount and hooked it. Louise tightened it to the back of the tractor and climbed into the seat. Sandy started the Plymouth and shifted it into reverse. Louise pulled the

32

chain taut, then paused. When she heard the V-8 start to wind up, she pulled forward steadily until the wagon was on level ground. Then she backed up a foot or two to put slack in the chain.

"Nice job, ma'am. You just won the tractor pull award of the day."

"I'd like to thank all the people who made my dream come true…" Louise knelt down and peered beneath the front bumper of the Plymouth. "Looks like the tie rod's sort of bent."

Sandy held the steering wheel to the left as he drove back up the hill. Louise had him drive it up onto the equipment trailer so they could check the front end. Besides the bent tie-rod, there was only a bit of body metal at the bottom of the fender that was curled under.

"I'm not too good with a torch." said Louise. "Are you?"

"No, I'm not."

"Well, Bob should be back shortly. He's the best welder around here."

"Say, that guy is a man of many skills. How old is he?"

"He's forty-one. You have to have a lot of skills to get by around here. Specialization only works when you've got a lot of people."

Sandy pondered the concept for a few minutes. "Tell me, Louise, how old were you when you learned about sex and reproduction and all that?"

"To be quite honest, I don't even remember. Growing up the country you just sort of know it because you see it happening in the everyday routine. You know that some of the critters are male and some are female. You know what they do and what the results are. That leaves only the details of the process, which you learn from other people. When you're around cattle and horses a lot, you're used to most of the males being neutered. I can remember at one point in my childhood being at a large gathering of people and wondering how to tell which of the men were the breeding stock and which were gelded. Of course, I assumed that all the women were breeding stock. It all seemed horribly unfair that there were so many women, with only a few 'bulls' to go around. It would mean that the only love you'd get was very fast and fleeting."

Sandy was laughing so hard his stomach was knotting up.

"You can imagine my relief to find out later that people just sort of blunder along on their own without any select breeding program."

Sandy caught his breath and added, "Imagine a kid's confusion now if they, first off, saw the cows being artificially inseminated." They were both laughing so hard there were tears.

Louise blurted out, "Now *that* would be horribly unfair!"

When Bob got back, they wheeled the gas bottles out to the equipment trailer. Bob heated on the tie rod while Sandy pounded on it with a hammer. It wasn't perfect, but it was functional enough for the rest of the trip to California. Next, Bob braised the strap back on the radiator. It looked like a professional job.

The Plymouth being roadworthy, Sandy went back to the house to call Barbara. She was home, and still waiting to hear form Stan. She would call him back around 11:00 Eastern Time. "Sorry, Sandy, that you have to wait around so long."

"Oh, no problem, I'm staying occupied. I got a temporary job as a cowhand" he replied.

"A Calahan? Is that somebody's name?"

"No, Barb, a cowhand. Like a gaucho."

"Groucho?"

"No, gaucho, like a cowboy."

"A cowboy? Well, whatever you're doing, you seem to be having a good time. Listen, I'll call you later. Just don't be hanging around the Long Branch, pardner."

Sandy laughed, "Ok, Barb, talk to you later."

"Bye, Sandy."

Sandy was chuckling as he hung up the phone.

"So, what's happening now?" Louise asked.

"She's going to call back at 9:00. Hope she's heard from Stan by then. So what are you up to?"

We've got to get most of what's left of the hay out so they'll give the grass a chance to grow out more. Also, there's a stretch of fence up on French Creek that's down."

I'll help any way I can." Sandy offered.

"Ok, why don't you and I work on spreading the hay, and Bob can go up to French Creek."

"Gotcha, pardner."

"Gotcha, what?"

Louise drove the 4-wheel drive pickup and Sandy, standing in the back, tossed the bales over the sides as they moved along. He learned very quickly that just standing up and throwing the bales was too physically exhausting to do for very long. It was much easier to slide the bales off over the sides of the pickup bed. After the first load they switched. Sandy felt a twinge of guilt to be sitting there idling along behind the wheel of a truck while this pretty, young woman did the hard work. He felt a soreness in almost every part of his body. He had never felt so exhilarated and so tired at the same time.

The sun was putting on another blazing sky show when they saw Bob come up over the top of a hill. He was riding Ferdinand. A big grin flashed across his face as he rode up. "You should have seen this old pony work a while ago. There was a baby calf limping along on three legs. I got up close and belly roped him. From then on, ol' Ferd kept the rope taut while I doctored the calf, and he circled back and forth and kept the old cow away 'til I was done."

Louise patted the old roan's neck. "Yeah, he's a good old horse. Aren't you boy?"

That night they ate a good supper. Two fried chickens, potatoes, string beans, and hot rolls with butter. Sandy started to say he would be leaving in the morning, but the words got stuck in his throat. He found himself saying, "That Ferdinand is a pretty smart old horse. Isn't he about as smart as they come?"

Louise nodded. "He's smart all right. That's for sure. But I know of one that was a little smarter. He's dead now, but while he was living, he amazed an awful lot of people."

"Including you?" Sandy asked.

"Especially me," she answered. "He was a bay gelding that started out life on the Front Range in Colorado.

"He was out of a grade mare by a remount stallion. So his sire was part of the US Cavalry. He was a bay, with a long back. As a colt he was more inquisitive than most. It was still very much winter on the eastern slope of Colorado and there was still snow on the ground. He was jumping into the patches of crusted-over snow- discovering everything his legs could do. Before the year was out he came into the possession of a woman they called Rattlesnake Sally. She was a small time rancher; small in stature, with an enormous amount of energy.

Some said she never actually gave him a name, but just called him 'Baby' or 'Sugar', and referred to him as 'that bay horse of mine'. He was the only horse on the place, so he received a great deal more attention than the average colt-in-training. She was more than just his trainer; she was feeder, groom, and companion as well, and he was completely devoted to her. Besides breaking him to lead and ride, she also taught him to count with his front foot and to maneuver himself so she could open and close gates without dismounting.

By the time he was a two-year-old, he was too tall for her to mount from the ground. She had to lead him alongside a fence or stump to climb into the saddle. According to more than a pair of witnesses, Sally would be in the house carving gunstocks, which kept her in groceries, when a cow would climb into the sheep pen. The bay horse would go and stand next to the stump and commence to snort and paw the ground until she arrived, bridle in hand, ready to re-segregate her livestock."

"It was common practice in those days for horses-for-hire stables to turn most of their stock loose in the wintertime to forage along the highway right-of-way and unfenced land. The nameless colt, who never found much difficulty finding his way out of nearly any enclosure, took to slipping out for a jaunt with these stray mustangs from time to time. He was always back by feeding time, though, sometimes bringing a lady friend or two along with him.

Sally decided it was time to have him gelded, and got a vet to do the job in exchange for an elk skin vest she made for him."

*This story first appeared in a Wichita, Kansas magazine- City Lights, in 1985.

"But he was a four-year-old by then, and sometimes when a horse is gelded that late in life, they never give up their mare chasing tendencies. Such was the case with Sally's horse. But he did become more of a homebody then, only slipping out once in a while- probably just for the hell of it."

"He was still a young horse when Sally died. People assumed she died of a heart attack- no autopsy was ever performed. She had no children. All her close relatives had died. There were only nieces, nephews, cousins and the like. So her estate was sold at auction. Every cow, sheep, gunstock, shovel, rake, rug, painting, and quilt. And along with the rest, a remarkably intelligent, young bay gelding- who up until then, had only been handled by Rattlesnake Sally.

When the gavel fell, the horse with no name became the property of one Bobby Brooks for the sum of $125.00. Bobby was a welder by vocation and a rodeo cowboy by avocation. It didn't take long for him to realize that his new acquisition had unusual qualities. If he was out in a pasture with anything to graze on, he was not about to be lured in by a bucket of grain. Sally could have walked up to him anywhere. But Sally was gone. And for him it was a whole new ball game. To catch this horse, he had to be surrounded to the extent that he could not run past a person close enough to be touched. That was the determining factor. It was a rule that always applied. Once he was caught, and had a saddle and bridle on him, he would do anything you asked of him. Bobby took to calling him 'Rattler' in honor of Rattlesnake Sally, and the name stuck. His initial venture into the realm of rodeo was in calf roping. Rattler had grown up with cattle and knew how to work them. The first time Bobby climbed on him, rope in hand, he knew what to do. What he didn't know was that the second the calf was caught, he had to stop, immediately, and back up to keep tension on the rope. It didn't take him long to learn, but the learning was painful. A sudden, unexpected blow to the head of a horse is as painful as it is to a man. To make things worse, several of Bobby's friends contributed to the training of the bay horse, and they usually had a beer or two before they got started. But in the final analysis, Rattler fared better than most others- he was quick to learn, and full of competitive spirit. Most of the boys agreed, 'He warn't no jughead.'"

"The bay's speed and prowess soon gained him a reputation. Bobby could rent him out to a couple of other ropers and barrel racers and come home with money in his pocket without even placing in the calf-roping himself. One man who was fascinated by the bay's ability was a self-taught saddle-maker named Wes George."

Sandy said, "Now hold on a minute. I don't understand this thing about catching a horse out in a pasture."

Bob explained, "Ninety-nine plus percent of horses, if you want to bring them to you, you simply put a handful of grain in a bucket, get their attention, shake the bucket, they walk up, they start eating the grain, you put your arm around their neck, slip a halter on their head and they're ready to cooperate with you. But the Rattler had this attitude, if there was anything else growing out of the ground he could chew on, it was 'I don't feel like it. Take your bucket and stick it on your head.' You've heard of attitude? That horse had it."

"Oh, ok, I think I understand." Sandy replied.

Louise continued. "Wes George had a talent for handling animals and a genius for leather carving. He was, perhaps, the first person to really appreciate the Rattler's intelligence. He was married, had two kids, and really couldn't afford what Bobby wanted for the bay horse. But he had a couple of nice used saddles, a pair of bronc spurs, and a disarmingly friendly stutter. He made the bargain for the equivalent of two hundred 1957 dollars.

"The long backed horse seemed to have a gameness and adaptability that was irrepressible. Next to the calf chute he was taut, but not tense. He crouched in the box like a baseball hitter. He pounced-out after the calf and caught it in a few strides. If you didn't have it laced up by then, you felt like a fool. To make matters more intense, if you didn't catch it, he'd bite the calf on the back just to show he'd been there.

"It was kind of a trade-off to him. 'I'll play your games, but you've got to play mine.' He never understood our rules. Why couldn't he run into that piece stretched across the front of the box? Why did they keep letting the calves go? He was put into a trailer, taken out of a trailer, saddled, bridled, handled, mishandled, borrowed, rented, fed and watered. He may have never understood, but he went through it with a predictably cool attitude. But what he did in his time off was, perhaps, a little too cool."

"By the time he was a six-year veteran of the road, he had walked cattle guards, crawled under fences, swum ditches, and opened latches, snaps, and baling wire loops all over eastern Colorado, southern Wyoming, and western Nebraska. He was lovable but exasperating. The little saddle-maker could put his three kids on him and turn his back without worrying about anything. He was never really sure how it happened, but somebody had gone overboard in teaching the bay how to keep the rope taut. One day Wes set out to trim his feet and tied the lead-shank to the fence. The bay immediately planted his back feet and heaved back with all his might. When the rope snapped he fell over backwards and lay still. Wes laid his head to the horse's rib cage. His heart was beating. He yelled to his daughter, Joan, to get a bucket of water. He felt for breath from the horse's nostrils. He was breathing. When Joan arrived with the water, Wes dumped it on the bay's head. In a few seconds he raised his head and looked around. Within a few minutes, he was on his feet. Wes heaved a sigh of relief. He never again tied any rope horse. The incident did nothing to lessen the Rattler's backing reflex, and quite a few people learned the hard way that he couldn't be tied. Drop his reins on the ground and he would never wander farther away than the next clump of grass.

"In the winter of 1958, Rattler got rented out to some of Wes's roping buddies. He was put in a stall inside an indoor arena in an area of Denver which had once been rural but had become surrounded by the city. He was being fed, along with a bunch of show horses, oats and molasses and South Park hay. The other horses dragged their hay out of the manger and slept on it. The Rattler ate every kernel of grain and every wisp of hay. He'd grown up in the hills and knew how short the food supply could be. But the quarters were too confining for his taste. So he sneaked out one night. No one knows for sure how he made the escape. One trick of his was witnessed by Wes George. He was in a barb wire enclosure. The bay looked along the lowest strand of wire until he found a low place in the ground below the wire. He laid down on his side, then he worked his neck and back until he slithered under the wire and he was outside the fence. But the escape from the indoor arena was never solved. He wound up on Federal Boulevard, munching weeds behind a fireworks stand. He had been free for several hours and the lights and the noise were starting to bother him. When two teenage boys in a pickup truck pulled up to the fireworks stand, he walked up and sniffed the tailgate. 'Hey, maybe he wants a ride.' one of them said, then he walked back and lowered the tail gate, saying, 'hop in fella.' to their amazement he did. They drove around for over an hour trying to find where their runaway belonged. Finally someone directed them to the indoor arena. The caretaker didn't even know a horse was missing. The main gate was still padlocked. A latch on the stall door that even small children couldn't open had been opened by a horse.

"The winter of '58 was long and hard. There was a recession going on. A cowboy named Jack offered Wes two hundred fifty dollars for his horse. By that time Wes had spent more than a couple of nights driving around trying to find his wandering gelding. Maybe it was his hormones, maybe it was just a game he loved to play. Anyway, it was exasperating.

"So a deal was made. Jack took the horse out to his place; Wes paid the rent, bought shoes for the kids, and got out of the red for the time being. But you don't forget a horse like that. Wes drove by Jack's place a couple of times just to take a look. The bay horse standing out in the snow-covered pasture looked thin and rough. He was surrounded by sheep fence, which, even for an escape artist like him was hard to negotiate. Besides that, there were no better pickings in the surrounding area. Wes knew the horse well enough to know he didn't waste any feed given to him. The little saddle-maker was at a loss for a solution. The money had been spent and getting it together again seemed hopeless. He kept from telling his family about it, but it bothered him constantly. Relief appeared in the form of a young doctor with a small piece of land in the foothills, and a modest income. A roper friend of Wes's introduced him to Dr. Walker at the western store one afternoon. The doctor wanted a horse that could keep up with his wife's paint mare, and that he could trust around his kids. Wes gave it to him straight. He didn't own the horse, but if 'Doc' wanted to advance him two hundred fifty dollars, he was sure he could get Jack to part with the bay gelding. He would even come by and shoe him, and the paint mare as part of the deal.

"That night, after supper, Wes left in the pickup. He put the money in an envelope and left it in Jack's mailbox. Then he pulled around by the county road in back of the pasture. He hoped to God that the bay wouldn't run from him and he didn't. Mainly he was hungry and Wes had always fed him well. Wes parked the truck by the fence corner. Rattler walked over and watched him as he untwisted the wire. Wes laid an arm over his neck and led him through. He dropped the tailgate and the bay jumped in. There was a wafer of alfalfa in the truck bed. The bay put one foot on the hay and bit off a mouthful. Wes smiled; that was too fine a horse for a damn fool like Jack.

"He drove a quarter mile before he turned on the headlights. Dr. Walker was waiting in the parking lot when he arrived at the western store. The Doc had borrowed a horse trailer, and bought a new halter and lead shank. Wes jumped into the back of the pickup and slipped the halter on Rattler, then jumped down and lowered the tailgate. The bay bent his head down and gauged the distance, then he jumped down. Wes grabbed the lead rope and led him to the back of the trailer. He tossed the lead rope across the horse's neck and he climbed in. "Well, Doc, he's all yours. I'll come around in the next few days to get him and your mare shod. I ain't makin' nothin' out of it, I just can't stand to see him abused." Dr. Walker assured him that he wouldn't be.

"At that time the doctor didn't really know what kind of an animal he had bought. He had seven children who would use him for everything from a pack horse, to a race horse, and a show horse to a living jungle gym.

"The youngest girl in the family was only a month or two old when the Rattler joined the family. But it was with her that he developed a special, personal communication that transcends the realm of conditioning and left many seasoned horsemen shaking their heads in disbelief. She started riding about the same time she started walking. She could walk up to the bay gelding anytime, anywhere. The mad, frenzied effort to escape didn't include visits from Rosetta; she was special. Maybe she was a lot like Rattlesnake Sally. Maybe he was just showing his appreciation of what he considered to be a well-trained

41

human. We'll never know

"The following spring brought a big change in the bay horse's life. The Walker family moved to Louisiana and he did too. The family had also acquired a brown, part Shetland pony. The pony, like many Shetlands, had a reputation for having a bad disposition. But the Walker kids weren't like most kids. They wouldn't put up with any dirty tricks and the pony had to mend his ways. He and the bay became fast friends. Most horses of small stature get picked on by their larger neighbors. Smoky never was again. Rattler defended him many times from the bullying of other horses. They were inseparable until the pony's death in 1966.

'"he bay's first residence in in Louisiana was at a boarding stable with some pasture, some Spanish moss covered trees, and a few oil rigs. There were thirty or so other horses there and there was always a certain amount of one-upmanship going on. The bay seemed to be vying for top horse. The lady who managed the place had a mare with lovely conformation and a sweet disposition. With a small crowd of onlookers she was demonstrating how she could open and close gates while remaining in the saddle. The mare got close enough to the gate that she could open the latch, push open the gate, then ride through, push the gate closed, and latch it from the mare's back. One of the Walker boys, mounted on old Rattler, waited patiently while the lady showed off for her audience. Then, without fanfare, the bay walked to the gate and held it with his right side, so the boy could unfasten it, pushed the gate open with his nose and walked through. Once there, he pushed the gate closed in the same manner, then held it with his right side while the boy closed the latch. The stable manager quickly lost her audience. She declared to bystanders that the bay was a good horse but the Walkers didn't train him. Another Walker, close at hand replied, "Nobody trained him to do that, ma'am, he just figured it out by himself." Later on the lady remarked that the Walker kids would be ok if they weren't such smart alecks.

"A year or so later, some of the horses at the stable became infested with lice. It was decided that the dipping tank would be filled with lice dip and the horses run through it. Many horses are somewhat squeamish about walking through water, but with the encouragement of many people, other horses, and the

42

occasional electric prod, most horses could be persuaded to jump into a dipping tank. The Rattler was always an exception. When his turn came to trot down the chute, he suddenly turned and climbed over the wooden fence and took off across the pasture at a lope. He was soon up in the trees and briar patches and it was getting late. The Walkers decided to wait until the next day when they could round up more people. The next day there were eleven Walkers and six other people on hand to try and dip the old gelding. One of the Walker kids led him into the chute; everyone else spread out along the fence and prepared to rebuff any attempt to climb out. But as soon as he was in the chute, he calmly jumped into the tank, swam across, and exited the other side. Some laughed, some frowned, some said, "I'll be damned." But they never could predict what he would do.

"During the sixties the Walker kids amassed a mantel full of trophies and ribbons from rodeos to shows and parish fairs. They were scrappy kids- some say spoiled brats- but they always showed due respect for the old bay horse that was largely the reason for their perennial success.

By the early seventies, the Walkers had moved to a three hundred acre farm with woods, fields, and a stream running through. The original plan was to put up a single electric wire around all the pastures. The Rattler, who was familiar with electric fences, would first nose the wire to see if it was on. Then he would retreat thirty or so feet, then make a mad dash for the wire, catching it at chest level and snapping it. He never went anywhere. He never let any of the other horses wander off. He just liked to break the wire. So, increasingly heavier gauges of wire had to be put up until they found one that was too heavy for him to break. People are still asking themselves why he would do such a thing.

"Life became simpler for the old gelding. He had wide green pastures with just a few trees. There was Spanish moss, which he had developed a taste for. Then there was only Rosetta, for the most part, to keep him in touch with the human race. He was in his late twenties when he died. Only a few other horses were around when it happened. Rosetta was walking the trail through the woods when she saw the buzzards circling. A few minutes later she had her shotgun and was running out the back door. Mrs. Walker caught up with her daughter at the edge of the south pasture. With tears streaming down her face she was picking off buzzards that were tearing the flesh from her favorite friend.

"The word passed along, eventually- to Colorado, Nebraska, Wyoming- all the places he'd been, all the people he's known. Most of them said, "Best damn horse I ever rode." And they meant it. Wes George poured a snort of whiskey for himself and one for his wife. "He was the best. Aggravating as all get out- he sure was a smart horse- and he weren't never abused."

"And go out west where the states are square."
Thomas Wolfe; Of Time and the River.

They had finished eating and were cleaning up when Louise's story ended.

Bob spoke: "A truly remarkable animal. Not just smart, but a very competitive athlete as well. Louise, should I tell him about the Judge?"

"Not if we're going to bed tonight." She turned to Sandy, "The Judge was a dog. He was always moving rocks, nobody knew why."

"Had a lot of other strange habits too." Bob said. "Nobody knew where he came from. Just sort of showed up at these people's place one day. Well, I guess I'll turn in. Goodnight." Bob headed up the stairs. Louise reached over and hooked a thumb under Sandy's belt.

"Yeah, the most amazing things just turn up at people's places."

"Yes...well." Sandy couldn't think of anything to say, then the phone rang. Louise answered it.

"Hello."

"Hi, this is Barbara, may I speak to Sandy Rose?"

"Hi, Barb, this is Louise. He's right here."

Sandy took the phone. "Hi, this is Sandy."

"Grab a pencil, I've got a whole list of instructions to give you."

"Ok, wait 'til I get situated." He found his note pad and a pencil, then sat down on the sofa. "Ok, shoot."

"When Stan found out he was in danger, he went to the FBI for help. Once he convinced them it wasn't a hoax, they agreed to help him. They sent him to a place called Pocatello, Idaho. You'll have to go there and report to the local sheriff. They'll screen you with some questions and then take you to Stan and Susan. That's about the size of it."

"The whole situation seems to be kind of shaky. I guess all we can do is hope for the best."

"Yeah. Actually I'm really relieved that at least they know what they're up against, and what they need to do about it."

"Sure, I am too. But what brought this whole thing about, anyway?"

"I don't know about a lot of the details, but basically what happened was this; Stan was writing a story on this crime syndicate. It was supposed to be with their knowledge. He had this paid informer he'd gotten this background from. Then one day he went to meet this contact and there was this other guy with him. This new guy starts demanding a percentage of the profits. Stan tells him there isn't any profit; it's not for a book, just newspaper articles. They got into an argument and the meeting ends without any agreement. The next thing Stan knows, this new guy is dead and his informant tells him the syndicate thinks Stan was in on it. That's when he went to the FBI for help. That's all he's told me so far."

"Well, I guess we'll just play along. What else can we do? Have you heard from Jake?"

"Only what Stan told me before."

"We'll hear from him eventually."

"Let me know as soon as you catch up with Stan."

"Yeah, as soon as I get to Pocatello and see the sheriff."

Sandy went out to the Plymouth and checked the tire pressure. He turned on the headlights. One front parking light was out, so he found a Phillips head screwdriver and removed the lens. He got a 12v bulb from Bob and replaced the one that was burned out.

He had laid awake the night before, for about an hour, reading Bob's poetry. It had been impossible to read it quickly. The images were bold and moving. The technique of expression was fresh—not imitative of anyone. Most of it was free verse, but with a definite rhythmic underpinning. Some of it was humorous, some tragic, but the themes were new and unusual. Louise tip-toed in while he was reading and sat down beside him on the bed.

"Want some company?"

Sandy smiled at her. "You bet," he answered, an expression he'd picked up from Bob. He thought of it as a colorful way to say yes. "Sit down here and hold my arm while I finish this page."

"You like it?"

"I like it. It's definitely distinctive. I wish I had more time."

"Why don't you take it with you, you can always send it back later on."

"He won't mind?"

"Nah, as a matter of fact I'm surprised that he let you read it. Most of his friends don't even know that he writes."

"I promise to take good care of it. Now, Louise, there's something I think we need to talk about." She didn't say anything for a moment.

Then she said, "I have the same feeling, but I don't know where to start. I can only say that, well, I've gotten attached to you."

Tears were starting to form in Sandy's eyes. He closed his eyes for several seconds. "I don't know how to put this... Do you remember that song from the sixties, 'We can work it out'?"

"I know, yes. But we've both got a big brother, and you're on a mission... But why don't we just say we'll stay in touch?"

"Well, yeah...we'll just stay in touch. Now crawl in here and let's get some sleep."

It was about an hour before they got to sleep, but it was a peaceful sleep.

The next day the Gages both left early to go after fencing supplies. Sandy took one last look around before he climbed in the Plymouth and headed south to the interstate.

His mind wandered back through the series of events that led up to his current predicament. At the center of the situation was the involvement with Stan. But he couldn't place any blame there. These things just happen. There was no use in looking back and saying, "I should have done this, or I should have done that." More important now was the question, "What do I do next?"

The issues at hand were; Stan was in hiding, but he and Susan were most likely ok, and Jake was somewhere in the Far East and he was ok too. So what was there to be done but chase the sun to the Northwest and listen to the tape-player? Willy was singing "... we come here quite often and listen to music, partaking of yesterday's wine." He decided that next chance he got he would Xerox Bob's poetry and send the manuscript back. He got a kind of mystical feeling from the big man's writing.

One of his poems said, "You've got to get down close to this country—where you feel the thin blades of grass push out through the gritty soil—breathe the sagebrush's earthy incense, and explore the rock haunts of the rattlesnake and the domain of the jackrabbit." It seemed to him that maybe what Bob Gage- no, Robert Gage, had to say, would appeal to a lot of people.

Louise parked the pickup in front of the cleaners. "How long will your haircut take?" she asked Bob.

"Shouldn't take too terribly long. Depends on who's ahead of me."

"I think I'll stay here and visit with Opal until you get back."

"Ok, I'll see you later."

The sign on the door said, "Worth's Cleaners- Yes we're open." Louise had known Opal most of her life. They'd been classmates in school since the third grade. Like Louise, Opal had been married and widowed. She had one son, Tom, who was sitting on a washing machine reading a Sports Illustrated when Louise came in.

"Hi, Louise," said Opal, "look who's here Tom." He grinned and waved at Louise. He was ten years old and had been deaf since birth. Although he was gradually learning to talk, he was hesitant to try it very often.

"Hi Opal, hi, Tom. How'd my blankets come out?"

"Real good. Did you guys get hit hard by that storm?"

"We lost eight baby calves that we know of. There's a few more that still have the sniffles, but other than that we didn't come out too bad."

"Glad to hear it. Tommie's teachers say he's coming along real well with his talking. He's still kind of shy about it- not too sure of himself, but he's getting there."

"Hey, that's wonderful." Louise responded. Tom grinned bashfully. He had grey-blue eyes and brown hair like his mother, and was slightly built for his age. The aptitude tests had shown that he had above average intelligence.

"They keeping you busy?" she asked Opal.

"Oh, not too bad. It should be picking up now that summer's coming. People bring in their stuff before they store it away for the summer. What's happening with you?"

"Met a real nice guy- quite by accident. City boy. Runs an import business in Virginia."

"Goodness, sounds intriguing. How'd you meet him?"

"His car got stuck during the blizzard. Bob found him and brought him up to the house. He's about thirty. His name's Sandy Rose."

"Well, if you don't have all the luck!"

"Oh, not really. He's driving across the country. He left this morning. I may never see him again, but maybe I will. Before he left he promised to keep in touch. It was just nice, for a change, to feel wanted."

"Yeah, I know what you mean."

When Bob arrived they were talking about horses. Both of Bob's ears were completely exposed. Opal made a comment to the effect that she hoped the weather stayed nice so he wouldn't lose them. Before Louise left, she invited Tom to come out some time and go riding.

On the way home, the conversation centered about their recent visitor.

"I wonder if we'll ever see him again," Louise commented casually.

"You seem to think I'll see my poetry again." Bob replied, grinning, "I think you'll see him again—the question is, do you want to?"

"Sure I do. Why, do you think I'm so love-starved from being out here so long that I've lost my senses?"

"No- I never knew you had any." Bob laughed uproariously and Louise punched him on the shoulder.

Louise asked, "Did you find anybody to come out and help us brand?"

"Yeah, a few local guys. Tom and Ed Gurn, Adam Hamber and Win Davis. Most of the Clayhorn boys. I guess we'll start out at the Penrose place, get it out of the way, then Mrs. Tober's place."

"Starting when?"

"Saturday at Penrose, Monday at Tobers. They'll each take only one day. Then start ours on Tuesday, do as much as we can, finish up sometime on Wednesday and go from there. Figure to go to Clayhorns next."

"How short-handed are we going to be?"

"Maybe not too bad. Bard Clayhorn recruited a couple of college kids from Ft. Collins to come out and help us. He claims they'll work hard. They haven't had much experience, but Bard said they're dying to learn."

"How much do we have to pay them?"

"Nary a nickel. Bard told them that all we could offer them was room and board, and they said that was fine. They want to do it just for the experience."

"Sounds like a hell of a deal."

Bob stopped at the mailbox and Louise got out for the mail. There were a few things addressed to 'box-holder' and a couple of bills. Louise climbed back in and stuck the mail in her purse. They drove toward the house, through the yard, and on to the northeast road. It was a few miles out that the fence was down. The property line actually ran across the side of a hill, but they had given up on making the fence follow that line. They had tried running the fence across the top of the hill, but there were rocks in the ground that prevented drilling post holes. So, they had finally decided to run the fence around the bottom of the hill. They were giving up an acre or so of area, but when you own sixteen sections, what does an acre matter?

Bob drove slowly along their planned fence line. Louise sat in the bed of the truck, and every time Bob stopped, she tossed out a post. They would come back later and work on setting the posts. The barbed wire they left in the truck bed. They would string the wire with the roll of wire in the truck and the loose end attached to a post. They had a few posts that were eight inches in diameter to provide the horizontal strength of the barbed wire fence.

The posts unloaded, they headed for a well that was close to their northeast section corner. The stock tank there had sprung a leak and needed repair. Louise climbed the windmill tower with the wrench in her back pocket. The structure was over thirty years old, but it had been kept in good condition and would be serviceable for a long time to come. In between breezy gusts, Louise stopped the propeller with a gloved hand and held it in place, while with the wrench in the other hand, she unbolted the shaft from the arm. When she released the propeller it spun freely in the breeze. She thought, "What a hell of a lot of free energy there is in the Nebraska wind."

50

When she'd climbed down from the tower, she and Bob tipped the oblong galvanized steel tank up on its side. Bob then maneuvered the pickup so that the bed was alongside the tank and about two feet away. One end of the tank was halfway along the length of the bed. Then they both got on one end of the tank and lifted it until it stood on end. Bob kept it balanced there while Louise got to the opposite side. Then they leant it over against the side of the pickup. Next, they lifted from the bottom end until the tank was lying across the bed of the truck. This done, they drove back down to the ranch house. Bob would later braise a sheet metal patch on the bottom of the tank without removing it from the truck.

Branding was a yearly event that was both festive and exhausting. It took lots of people, lots of horses and lots of equipment. There was a lot more to it than just branding. Male calves had to be castrated and there were vaccinations to be given. Some ranchers notched ears and some used ear tags. Most used portable butane stoves or gasoline stoves to heat the irons. For a herd the size of the Gage's, it took about forty people and twenty or so horses. That required mountains of food for both men and mounts. It took about forty pickups and a dozen or more horse trailers. It took syringes and other veterinary supplies, disinfectants, hundreds of feet of rope, electric prods, and insect repellant—as well as cases of beer, bottles of whiskey, and countless cans of snuff and plugs of chewing tobacco.

Louise spent most of the day Monday getting food ready for the following day. Chili was a popular main dish for lunch on branding day. It was inexpensive, fairly easy to make, and most of the cowboys liked it. The general rule was that the host outfit put out the main dish and the visitors brought along such things as salads, vegetables, bread, and desserts. Louise, however, prided herself on her baking ability and she had a dozen loaves of home-made bread included in her menu, as well as a half-dozen cherry pies.

Bob, meanwhile, was finishing up the fence repair on the northeast section. He used a post-hole auger that ran off a three-quarter inch, heavy-duty hand drill. The drill was powered by a voltage converter which was, in turn, powered by the engine of his truck. He was pleased to find that he hit very few rocks in drilling his holes. Once or twice he hit some medium sized cobbles, but by starting his hole a little to one side or the other, he got around them without any problem.

Once he had the holes drilled, he removed the loose soil with a post-hole tool, commonly referred to as a 'post-hole digger.' An English teacher would be quick to point out that the 'digger' was the person operating the tool, and not the tool itself, which was a digging tool.

Bob always used four strands of barb wire, evenly spaced. Some ranchers used five strands with uneven spacing, some only used three. Bob liked to leave eighteen inches from his bottom strand to the ground. This left enough space so that antelope or people could crawl under the fence. It was much better than having people climb your fence and made it easier for antelope to get around. Antelope don't have the leaping ability of deer and elk. Their natural habitat is open country which doesn't have the natural barriers of woodlands and the jumping ability wasn't an evolutionary necessity. Cattle, as well as bison, can't do either, so wire fencing is an effective barrier method. This is why deer and antelope have been able to thrive in those wilds, still left amid domesticity, while the bison have had to be domesticated to even survive.

Both Bob and Louise were up as the first streaks of sunlight hit the tops of the cottonwood trees. Their neighbors would be arriving soon. Bob had his five riding horses in the corral next to the barn, and they had been given a generous ration of oats and molasses, as they would be putting in a hard day's work. He'd checked their feet, all twenty of them. Copper had a pebble stuck under the shoe of his right front foot. The buckskin horse had some loose nails on his back shoes, which he had to reset. The rest were ok.

Winchester Davis was the first to arrive. He parked his faded blue pickup next to the barn and went out to help Bob. He had no horse of his own, and would be riding one of Bob's. They had competed together in team roping since they were teenagers. Win had owned several horses in the past, which he usually kept at Bob's place since he lived in town then. His saddle and gear were also at Bob's place.

"Well, mornin' Win."

"Mornin' Bob. You got my horse saddled up for me already?"

"Nope, thought I'd leave that for you."

"Oh, how come?"

"I figured a first-class horseman such as yourself would want to personally see to the preparations himself."

"Ordinarily I would, but I'd trust you, Bob, you know that. Who should I ride, ol' buddy?"

"Why don't you ride the buckskin? We'll leave Ferd for one of Bard's college boys."

"Can they even ride a horse?"

"Bard says they can. They've all got horses of their own at home."

"Where are they from?"

"Denver and the Springs, mostly."

The buckskin was still chewing on his grain as Win laid the saddle across his back and cinched it loosely into place. He slipped the headstall and reins over Buck's head and let it hang around his neck. After he finished eating, Win would put the bit in his mouth and tighten his cinches.

"Yeah, Win, we don't know if these drugstore cowboys can work or not until we see for ourselves."

"If Ferdinand throws a fit we'll know just about what the rider knows."

"Yep, that's just about right. We'll know then."

The yard was filled with pickups, cars, and trailers as Bob and Win led their mounts out of the barn. A circle formed around Bob. He hunkered down to sketch out his directions on the ground.

"This area right up north here is where the catch-pen's at. We need to split up into three groups. There's two bunches of cattle we'll work today. We need about eight herders in each group. We need to bring this bunch from down south, and move them around by here and up to the catch-pen. The other bunch, up on Snake Creek, we need to spread out fairly well and circle them in, then bring them down along the creek. Everybody else will go with me. We'll need about three vehicles and get set up by the catch-pin, with our propane stoves and what not. Adam, why don't you head up the guys to go south, and Dave Clayhorn, head up the bunch to go up Snake Creek. Bard, why don't you let one of your guys go with Adam, and one with Dave, and you and the other guy go with me."

Bard Clayhorn and one of his buddies walked up to Bob as the three crews set off for their destinations.

"Bob, this is Ty Lester. He owns this outfit, Ty."

"Yeah, me, my sister and the Sandhills Bank and Trust own this place. Have you worked around stock much, Ty?"

"Just in rodeos, until we worked over at the Tobers' yesterday."

"So, at least you've got the gist of what's going on. Why don't you ride up with me and Sis, and Bard can ride with Win."

Ty was tall and thin, with blond hair and a disarmingly friendly smile. He climbed in after Louise and they rattled off up the road to the catch pen.

"What kind of schooling are you into Ty?" Louise asked.

"Journalism. I want to do newspaper or magazine work, and do some freelancing on the side. I've always liked rodeo, and since I'll probably never be a big star at anything, I want to write about the people and the sport and the animals from an insider's viewpoint."

"Well, Bob's about one of the best team-ropers in Nebraska and he does writing too."

"Now, Sis, you know what I told you about giving out family secrets."

"What kind of stuff do you write about?" Ty asked.

"Oh, some poetry, a few essays."

"Glad to hear it. I'd like to see it if I could."

"Louise, here loaned it to a travelling salesman."

Louise grinned, "Oh, hey, I didn't tell you. Sandy just called from Wyoming. He sent your poetry back and he's doing fine. Still hasn't heard from his brother."

"That's good to hear." Bob turned to Ty, "If it gets back while you're still here, you're welcome to see it, if you promise not to laugh."

"Hey, why should *I* laugh? Are you a header or a healer?"

"Header. Win Davis is my heeler."

At the catch pen, Bob divided his work crew into jobs. Holders were in charge of holding the calves down. There were two on each calf. One held a knee on the calf's neck with a foreleg in his hand. The other held the upper hind leg and kept a foot on the other leg above the hock. No rope would be on the calf once the holders had it down, and they had to keep it down while shots, branding and castration were completed.

The cutters were old, experienced hands who worked quickly and cleanly, and could have the operation done in seconds.

Branders had to keep the irons hot and cleaned of debris to enable them to get the job done with a minimum of trauma to the animal. Win Davis, who had grown up around his father's welding shop, had made Bob's current 'G' irons out of angle iron and rebar. Bob's father had formed the whole letter with a continuous line from a running iron. The new irons made the job easier and quicker.

Bob put himself in charge of shots. He carried a small can of spray paint with him to mark the calves that had been injected. The shot was the only step in the process where it wasn't apparent by looking at the calf if it had been attended to.

When they arrived at the catch pen, Bob motioned with his arm for the rest of the crew to follow him to the south. Ty jumped out and opened the gate and Bob led them to the north end of the pen. Tailgates were lowered on three vehicles and propane stoves were set up. On the tailgate of another vehicle, Bob set out bottles of mixed vaccines for the common bovine diseases. There were also disinfectants, several types of knife sharpeners, antibiotics and various topical ointments for treating wounds, and cancer of the eye.

Adam's bunch were the first to arrive. Before they came into view there was the sound of bleating from the calves and the occasional deep bawl of a mother cow. The cows came in view first, followed closely by their bewildered offspring trotting along in the trail of dust trying to find their dams. The lead herders kept them aimed towards the catch pen, while riding slowly and cautiously to avoid spooking the cattle. Four more men brought up the rear, and five bulls tagged along behind. The bulls knew that what was happening did not require their

their presence. Nonetheless, they felt prompted by nature to keep an eye on what was happening with their heifers.

Ty wanted to rope and so did Bard, so Bob let Ty use Ferdinand. Louise was going to rope for a while, then head back right before lunch. There would inevitably be some detail of the kitchen operation which was overlooked and for which Louise would have to be consulted.

Dave Clayhorn and his bunch arrived shortly after the first bunch had arrived. Soon they had about two hundred fifty cows milling around at the south end of the catch pen. Louise and Copper crept coolly in among the herd until they were within spitting distance of a calf. Louise let her loop drop easily around the calf's head and pulled up the slack. Soon she was pulling the bawling animal, who hopped stiff-legged in futile resistance, over to the vicinity of the holders. Two veteran hands quickly threw the calf to the ground and removed the rope. Louise coiled it up and went back for another calf. By then, Bard and Ty had each gotten a calf in tow. It wasn't long before everyone in the crew was moving around and performing his duty in the process. All morning long, Bob was hurrying from one animal to the next, vaccinating and occasionally giving antibiotics. By the time noon rolled around they had branded over fifty calves. Some were only a week or so old. By the time they were full-grown, the 'G' brand would be ten inches or more in diameter as the brand grew with the animal.

Most of the crew were enthusiastic with Louise's chili and homemade bread. Mrs. Tober's apple cobbler was also well-received. It was amazing to Bob, how much food could be put away by a bunch of cowboys once they were given the opportunity to do some exhausting work. Branding time brought an upbeat feeling to most of the ranchers. They were looking at new stock on the hoof. The new baby calves were the result of the same replication that kept the whole living world going; the miniature cow-critters came sliding into the world- the combination of DNA from the bull and the cow-from where only their mother knew and only their owner cared; up until the day they became officially recognized as an asset on the ledger sheet. Today they became identified and counted as full-fledged members of the bovine race- destined to become animal protein for consumption by the human race. This chili contained the fat and muscle of past baby calves that became incorporated into the bodies of living breathing human beings and enabled those humans to move and function in such a way as to allow more cows to eat more grass to become more cow; to become more human; to eat more cow.

The sun was straight up in the sky; daily moving north. The ground was a carpet of short green grass, with patches of bare ground in places where the elevation changed. The hills were like huge haystacks around them in three directions. From the air, they were like moguls on a ski slope but thousands of times larger. Grass grows abundantly on the sides of hills like these, whereas any other crop would require plowing. Plowing effectively reduces the surface area to the same as flat country. A cow can stand, or lie, on the side of a hill just as easily as on level ground; and they also seem to know just when to face uphill at just the right times. To plant a hill's surface would require terracing. A terrace is parallel to the surface of flat land. On a terraced hill, all the plants grow on the horizontal surface. The vertical area doesn't count.

The sky was a bottomless blue. (It might as well have been topless). The clouds were high, white, and drifting. It was one of those memorable days when the air was cool- the breeze just strong enough that, in the sun, it was just warm enough, and in the shade, you felt cool as a tall glass of water from the bottom of the well.

The Gages had four wells on their land, but they weren't artesian wells. Fossil water lay thousands of feet underneath most of the sand-hills. Artesian water, and self-propelled sprinkler systems, had transformed much of the semi-arid hills, which before could not be irrigated, into productive farmland. But when the water is gone, it can't be replaced. The Gage's wells were much shallower, and fed by precipitation. Using electric pumps and windmills, they were able to supply water for themselves and their animals, as well as irrigate a forty-acre alfalfa field. The alfalfa was watered by a system of aluminum pipes, which slid on runners and were towed behind a tractor from one place to another.

This forty acres of alfalfa was along Snake Creek and was the only ground they had which was anywhere near flat enough to grow a row crop. The rest of their land was much too hilly.

Their stomachs full, most of the hands were sitting under the trees, or standing by their horses, their cheeks full of Copenhagen and Union Standard, talking about their wives, their horses, their dogs, and kids, or their pickups. As Bob got up and moved toward his truck, the others stood and stretched, tightened their cinches, started their engines and the afternoon's work got underway.

By two o'clock they began letting some of the cows and calves that had been branded out of the catch pen to make it easier to find the remaining head. By four o'clock, Louise was the only one roping calves. The rest of the crew pitched in on the few remaining chores. Ty Lester was helping her by keeping the one calf they were after, separated from the rest.

"Finding anything romantic about this work?" she teased him.

"Oh, sure! I admit it is exhausting, but what is there worth doing that doesn't come without hard work?"

"I say, is that Descartes?"

"Yeah, I guess. Just don't get it before da horse!"

Louise broke into laughter. "Heh, heh, heh- Ty, you just made my whole day. I'll have to remember that one for posterity."

The wind was starting to kick up out of the southwest. A couple of hats were quickly tossed up into the wind currents. A big calf that had been pinned down by three men was finally released. As he rolled up on his haunches, he let out a bawl, then climbed to his feet and scampered towards the herd. A man who had just lost his hat called out, "That's just how I feel about it, sweetheart."

Things were working out better than they'd expected. They had all the Gage's new calves, as far as they knew, branded. Bob figured there might be a few somewhere they'd missed, but he and Louise could take care of those on their own. As they were getting their gear squared away, the ranchers plotted their strategy for the next few days. They would head out for the Clayhorn place in the morning. A truckload of Mexican longhorn bulls had arrived there recently. These were not part of their market or breeding cattle, they were strictly for recreational purposes. They would be used throughout the summer for jackpot steer roping and team roping. The plan was to get these animals castrated as quickly as possible, so that they sufficiently recovered by the weekend so they could be roped and tied without undue stress.

Many people, ranchers included, frowned on steer roping and did not participate in the practice. The sport calls for one horse, one rider, and one steer. The steer must be roped by the horns and jerked to the ground with the rider still mounted. Steers' necks are broken quite often in the process. Steer ropers are quick to point out that, were these animals not used for roping, they would wind up as fighting bulls in the arenas of Mexico. Interestingly enough, team roping, which is very easy on the steers in comparison, originated in the ranching practices of Mexican cattlemen, whereas, steer roping originated in the methods of Anglo ranchers. Without condemning or sanctioning either bull fighting or steer roping, it's a question of debate about which is more sporting.

Los toros taken care of, they could move on to branding the Clayhorn calves, which would include ear-notching this time, and of which there would be some two thousand head. They would do as many as they could get to by Saturday noon, then knock off until Monday. There would be a dance, complete with Western swing band on Saturday night at the Legion Hut in Valentine, Nebraska. Admission would be free; paid for by the Clayhorn Land and Cattle Co. On Sunday there would be jackpot roping and barbecue at the Clayhorn Ranch.

The Clayhorn spread covered ninety square miles, which they either owned or leased. Most of it was good grazing land, some of it was irrigated from the Ogallala aquifer. They had several gas wells which were leased to an energy company. Bard was the youngest of his generation and also the biggest. He stood six and a half feet tall and weighed in excess of two and a quarter. His great grandfather founded the company in 1913. He had aunts and uncles who were younger than himself. At the age of thirteen he was already competing as a steer and calf roper. By his soft-spoken and easy-going manner, and simple clothing, the casual observer would never guess he was from a family of multi-millionaires.

Bob was up early the next morning, getting ready to head for Valentine. Louise would stay and look after things until the weekend.

"Are you taking two horses up?" she asked.

"Yeah. Ferd and Buck; they're the ones we're going to rope off of."

"I was thinking, if you wanted, I could bring them up with me on Saturday. You know, just to keep there from being too many strange horses together."

"In that new building the Clayhorns put up, there are box stalls all around the outside. Those two could even be in one stall if necessary. But I think it might be better for Win and me to be on our own horses for a few days. That way, when we get in and start roping, we'll feel more in control, and maybe a little faster."

"Sounds reasonable. But that still leaves me without a trailer."

"There's going to be at least two dozen people heading up there on Saturday. Surely somebody will give you and Copper a ride up."

"Shirley Somebody? I don't think I know her." Louise grinned. "Do we stand out by the highway and try to hitch a ride?"

"You pick up the phone, smart ass, and call people and ask them. I don't know why it's so important. You'll only be using him for sixteen seconds."

"Yeah, but if I use some other horse, it could take a minute and a half! And tires only go flat on the bottom, right?"

"Well, sure!"

Louise could see there was no point in arguing at that point, so she changed the subject. "You eating chili for supper?"

"Do I have a choice?"

"Sure, you can have it plain or with cheese on top. Hot or cold. With crackers or..."

"Never mind, Cheese on top will be fine. With a tortilla."

"Can I maybe talk you into letting me use your Walkman while you're gone?"

Louise got to Valentine at eleven AM Saturday, along with Dr. Bill Fisher, a veterinarian from North Platte, his wife Sonja, and Tommie Worth. Louise had taken the liberty of inviting the Fishers along. They had a nice new Ford pickup and a two-horse trailer, so there was transportation for Louise's horse, and no one would complain about bringing along a vet.

Opal let her bring Tommie along even though they knew he might run into teasing from the other kids. He'd have to face it sooner or later, and this was as good a time as any. Besides that, the kid was crazy about horses. There would be break-away roping for the kids on Sunday and it would give him a chance to show the other kids what he could do. In break-away roping, the tail end of the rope was not tied around the horn, but was attached to it by a piece of kite string so that when the calf was caught, the rope would break free from the saddle and be dragged by the calf.

There were horse trailers galore in the yard at the Clayhorn place. A white horse was being shod beneath a cottonwood tree in the middle of the yard. Bard Clayhorn was holding the lead shank as the farrier worked. When Dr. Fisher pulled up, Bard let the lead shank drop to the ground and walked to the driver's window.

"Hi, I'm Bard Clayhorn. Well hello, Louise." he said.

"Hi, Bard," said Louise, "This is Doc Fisher and his wife Sonja."

"Glad to meet you. Going to rodeo with us tomorrow?"

"You bet," answered Louise. "What are you up to?"

"Most everybody's gone, taking the last bunch of cattle up to the old Brewster place. Dave and I were just about to go down and check on those longhorn steers."

Dr. Fisher said, "Why don't you wait a second and let us unload this horse, and we'll come along with you."

"Great, just pull up by that new building and stick him in any stall you can find. Dave should be here pretty quick."

She backed Copper out of the trailer and put him in a stall along with a big chunk of alfalfa.

"Who's Dave?" Sonja asked Louise.

"His dad. There are so many Clayhorn kids around here, they took to calling their first names just to avoid confusion. Bard is Dave's only kid, but he has lots and lots of cousins."

Dave Clayhorn was shorter than his son by four inches but the broad back and big hands were unmistakably alike. Louise introduced the Fishers before they all piled into a muddy blue Blazer with "Clayhorn Land and Cattle Co." painted on the door. Tommie tugged on Louise's sleeve and signed, "Where are we going?"

She looked into his face and slowly said, "To look at the steers."

Dave looked back over the front seat and asked, "Is that your helper?"

Tommie immediately nodded his head.

Dave added, "If anybody gives you any trouble, little buddy, you just tell me and we'll whip their butts."

Tommie grinned and whispered, "Ok."

The Mexican steers were undoubtedly eating better than they ever had. They were penned in the area that would be used for the jackpot roping on Sunday. The arena hadn't been used since the previous summer and had grown up in weeds, primarily kosha- the plant that, in the fall, became the familiar tumbleweed. Cattlemen sometimes bale the hardy weed for hay when facing hard winters, when better fodder is in short supply. The wonderful digestive system of the bovine harbors a bacterium which can convert cellulose into starch, which ultimately becomes beef.

As the blue Blazer pulled up next to the arena, the Clayhorns' new steers were lying down in the weeds, chewing their cuds. Observation of the second-time-around chewing process of the bovines must have had a profound effect on some people. Mothers and grandmothers, down through the ages, have been known to exhort small children to 'chew your food well, dear.' Presumably, this elaborate digestive system made it possible for the ruminants to eat quickly out in the grassy fields and then return to the safety of the forest to do their heavy chewing. After the group had leaned on the fence and observed for several minutes, Dave Clayhorn suggested, "Lets run 'em down and out through the chutes so we can look 'em over."

Bard and Louise proceeded to circle around to the other side while Dave trotted down to open the gate to the chute. With whistles and yips, the steers were driven into the holding pen.

"Looks like they've got good horns on 'em."

"Yep, pretty good horns."

One by one, they were forced into the chute. One of their Hereford bulls would not have been able to pass through such a narrow chute, but the Mexican cattle had no such problem. Through the spaces between the boards, Doc and the others carefully examined the scrotal area of the animals for swelling or hemorrhaging.

"That 'un's got good horns."

"Yeah, skinny neck, but good horns."

"They all got good horns."

"That 'un looks like he's swole up, sorta."

"Naw, I think he's all right. We'll see if he acts stiff when we run 'em out."

The mechanical gate flew open and the steer bolted out into the open.

"He don't act stiff."

"Yeah, he's all right."

One by one, the animals were let out of the chute. They all seemed to be healthy enough for the jackpot the next day. As they drove back to the Clayhorn place, Bard, once again, remarked, "Good horns on 'em."

In events where steers are roped, horns are vitally important. The animal can't be roped by the neck like calves are. Calves are small enough that being jerked by the neck usually won't do any harm. With an adult animal, the rope must fall either just around the horns, or around one horn and the nose, or 'half-head.'

The size and the shape of the horns is also important. Ideally the horns should be two inches or more at the base and extend laterally from the head so the tips are eighteen or more inches apart. Mexican cattle are bought selectively on that basis and the same qualities are desirable for steer wrestling. Calves for sport roping are usually Brahma or part-Brahma. Brahmas are hardy, tough, and resistant to injury. They are often hard to throw and tie, which adds to the competitiveness of the timed event. A good roper, who could rope and tie a

Hereford calf in twelve seconds, would take fourteen seconds to rope and tie a Brahma of the same weight.

Team roping requires two horses, two riders, and a steer. The steer is released, the riders pursue. First, the header ropes the horns, then turns his horse and begins to tow the steer. The heeler rides up from behind and ropes the hind feet by throwing the loop in front of the hind feet so the animal steps into it. Points are lost if only one foot is caught. Of all roping competition, team roping causes the least trauma on the cattle.

Of all the lunch-time spreads at any occasion, in any part of western Nebraska, none were as big as noon chuck at the Clayhorns at branding time. The motto was "all you can eat", and some of the boys did exactly that. There was chili. There was also chicken. There were calf fries and bull fries. There were five different kinds of beer on ice. For dessert, there was berry pie, Apple pie, cherry pie, peach cobbler, ginger bread, brownies, chocolate pudding, and home-made ice cream. After all that, there was 'smokeless tobacco'; just a pinch between you cheek and gum, or maybe a wad the size of a hen's egg.

Louise was talking to Sonja, who tended to stay pretty close at hand, when she heard retching and spitting accompanied by laughter from the other side of a Miley trailer off to her left. She surmised rather quickly what was taking place. Teddy Shoemaker, Clayhorn's version of Eddie Haskell, had talked Tommie into taking a big bite of his Beech Nut scrap for the amusement of the other kids. He hadn't bothered to tell him not to swallow the juice. When Louise appeared, Teddy decided it was time to leave, but as he turned, he ran smack into Bard Clayhorn. Bard grabbed one arm and Louise grabbed the other, and they proceeded to escort T.S. Shoemaker Jr., kicking and yelling in the direction of the water trough. He was crying, "Daaa-dy!" at the top of his lungs, while the cowboys roared with laughter.

T.S. Shoemaker Sr.'s only comment was, "Don't holler at me, son, I told you not to pull no stunts up here, but you wouldn't listen." Louise and Bard stuck his head under for the count of three, then let him go. Then his old man made him go sit in the pickup until it was time to go.

"Oh you can't expect a cowboy to agitate his shanks
In etiquettish manner in aristocratic ranks
When he's always been accustomed to shake the heel and toe
At the rattlin' ranchers' dances where much etiquette don't go."
                    James Barton Adams

Bradley Garrett and his Western Swing Band had played at the American
Legion Hall in Valentine on fourteen different occasions. They had played at the
Clayhorn's gathering the last six years in succession. The Legion Hall had a pretty
large dance floor and the stage went from wall to wall, plenty big enough for a
nine piece band.

The bar, manned by the Legionnaires in their overseas caps, was in the rear.
The variety of booze wasn't much, but it was moderately priced and there was
plenty of it. Most of the boys, however, did their drinking out of long neck
bottles in the parking lot.

Bradley played most of the popular C&W tunes, past and present, a selection
of Bob Wills' songs, and even a song or two by the Beatles and Jim Croce. Every
once in a while a car or pickup would head up the road, then twenty minutes
later would pull back into the parking lot. Anybody might assume they were out
smoking "them funny cigarettes", but the town marshal was hanging around the
parking lot all night, so it didn't really matter.

That night, the band started out their first set with "Livin' on Tulsa Time" and
ended up with "San Antonio Rose." While the band took a break, Bob set off to
find Ty Lester. Ty had mentioned a couple of days ago about embryo transplants
being researched at C.S.U.

"Those other two guys who came up with me, Waldo and Monty, they could
tell you more about it than I could. Basically what happens is they give a cow a
big dose of hormones and she ovulates a bunch of eggs all at once. Then they
fertilize them and keep them frozen until they've got their cow they want to
implant. So far they're getting good results. Monty and Waldo are both animal
science majors and they're pretty much up on the subject. What interests me, is
that you can mix them any way you want, and never have to transport them

anywhere. You could have, for instance, a pure bred Charolais cow. You get your semen sent to you from, say, a Brahma bull. Then you get your cow to ovulate and fertilize the eggs with the Brahma semen. Now you've got six or eight embryos you can sell to a dairy farmer, say, and he can implant his Holstein cows. Then, if he wants to, he can fatten these Charbray calves; and, he's got these super milk-producing cows for nurse cows and a lot of hybrid vigor in his calves."

Bob said, "And a guy wouldn't even have to fool with keeping a bull."

"Or pure bred cows, either."

"Sounds very interesting."

Right about then, Louise showed up accompanied by Sonja Fisher. "Well I finally caught up with you," she said to Bob. "Sonja, this is Ty, and I don't remember this other dude's name."

Sonja laughed, "Yeah, but he's got a sister who's a real space cadet. What happened to the Worth boy?"

"It's the funniest thing," Louise said, "Dave told him he could stay up at his place and I told him he could stay with Jim and Angie's kids at their place, which is where I'm staying. So, do you know where he wanted to stay?"

"I'll never guess."

"He wanted to stay in the barn with the horses, and sleep on the hay." Bob and Ty broke out laughing.

"So...ho, ho...ha, ha, ho... so where did he wind up?"

"He went home with Jim and Angie's kids. They were going to play Dungeons and Dragons until they fall asleep."

"I hope he's up and ready when we get ready to rodeo tomorrow."

"Well, he's not getting liquored up like the rest of us are."

"True, true," Bob admitted, "But us boys can hold our liquor. Sonja, do you know how these country girls hold their liquor?"

Louise interrupted them quickly, "Never mind, you don't want to know. Anyway, how would you know, you ain't even dancin' with anybody."

"There ain't nobody to dance with!"

"Where have you been looking? Oh, by the way, your stuff came in the mail."

"What stuff?"

"The stuff you told me not to talk about in public."

"Oh, my poetry. I tell you people, this woman has a genius for talking in riddles. Well, good. Ty will have a chance to read it before he leaves. Where is it?"

"In Doc's pickup."

Ty interrupted, "Oh say, there's Mondo and Wally now. Hey, come here a second, you guys. Bob here wants to know more about embryo transplants."

Monty walked up. "What do you want to know about it? I don't know that much, myself."

"Well," Bob said, "to start with, how much deleterious effect is there on the cow that the eggs come from?"

"None," Waldo said, "that I know of. The most potential for harm is in implanting the other cow."

Monty said, "There is going to be a conference about A.I. and E.T. at C.S.U. the first week in August. Sponsored by the A.B.B. and C.S.U.R.F."

"Sounds like you're talking about alphabet soup," Louise commented.

Waldo continued, "Yeah, Bob, you ought to take a few days off and come out for the conference. You'd learn a lot."

"You could stay at our place," Monty offered, "Ain't nothin' fancy, but you're welcome."

"I'll have to think about it," Bod said, "but it sure sounds like it could be really worthwhile."

"Sure, Bob," Louise urged, "it's just what you need. Get away for a few days and learn how to make test-tube heifers."

"Yeah," Waldo said, "you could be the fairy godfather of the cowboys."

Sonja joked, "The t bone of the immaculate conception."

Tommie Worth was awake at six AM. He picked up his clothes from the end of the bed and crept out into the kitchen. No one else was up. Quickly he slipped into his shirt and Levis, and pulled on his boots. From the coat rack by the kitchen door, he retrieved his coiled up nylon rope. The rope was stiff and very springy. Its surface was fuzzy from years of wear.

Out in the backyard, Tommie laid his rope down on a bale of alfalfa and went to get a bucket from the tack room. Placing the bucket bottom-side up on the ground, about eight feet from the bale, he spread the coils of rope evenly and held them between thumb and forefinger of his left hand. With his right hand, he pulled his hondo around in a circle towards himself. One and a half revolutions made the loop about three feet in diameter. This was the size he wanted, so he held the loop at the hondo and whirled it back over his right hand. Then he adjusted his grip about eighteen inches back from the hondo, holding his loop and lead together. With his loop 'built', he climbed atop the hay bale and whirled his loop, letting his wrist rotate in a circle centered by his right ear. In a graceful motion, he threw loop at the bucket as though he had thrown a rock. The loop landed just a little off center, and when he pulled up the slack, it lifted from the bucket. 0 for one. He reached out an arm's length with his right hand and held the rope, spun the loose end overhand, and made a coil. He repeated the process until his rope was neatly coiled. Then he built and threw again. This time his loop lay flat on the ground surrounding the bucket. He pulled back his slack and the bucket rose a few inches off the ground and landed with a clank. Tommie smiled. He was one for two. He tried again and again. At first his attempts were about half successful. But as he warmed up, he began to hit on almost every throw. It was about two and a half hours until cowboy Jim Tisch tapped him on the shoulder. He looked back at Jim, who patted his stomach and said, "Hungry?"

Tommie nodded then held up an index finger and whispered, "One more." He swung his loop for two revolutions and threw. Instantly he pulled back and the bucket rose a foot off the ground. He grinned and looked at Jim, who was clapping his hands enthusiastically.

Jim's son, Jeff, was a year older than Tommie, and his daughter, Ida, was a year younger. They liked having company, and Ida had dug her magic slate out of the toy cupboard right away. With this line of communication open, they got along royally. Jeff and Ida tended to be a bit patronizing, but compared to the alienation he often encountered, it was like heaven. They were both still in their pajamas and Angie was passing out the flapjacks when Jim and Tommy came in.

Jim said, "Tommie's been putting in a lot of practice time while you two were still sleeping."

"Well, he's going to need practice if he's beat me," Jeff boasted.

Ida wrote something on the magic slate and Tommie responded. Ida said, "Tommie says he's going to beat everybody."

"Everybody but me," Jeff insisted.

"Don't talk with food in your mouth," his mother said.

Ida was writing again on the slate. "All right," said Jim, "Let's hold off writing until we're done with breakfast."

"But Dad, how else can we talk to Tommie?"

"You don't need to talk right now, just remember what you have to say until we're done eating. Louise, did you want to get over there kind of early so you can practice a few times?"

"No, I never practice with them once they're trained. Just makes 'em nervous."

"Huh, I never knew that," said Jim, "Does it make 'em sour?"

"Yeah, they start knocking over barrels, slipping, that sort of thing. I never use a bat either. They're already at full stride. The bat just makes them nervous.

"I guess she would know," Angie said, "all those buckles and sadlles..."

"Just two saddles," Louise said modestly.

"Just two!" Angie exclaimed, "You kids want more pancakes?"

Louise looked at Tommie so he could see her lips move. "More pancakes?" she said with exaggerated enunciation.

Tommie held up one finger. Angie lifted the plate, "One more? Ok."

The usual procedure for jackpot roping was to start out with calf roping, then team roping, followed by barrel racing and break-away for the kids. Then, if time permitted, there would be another round of one or more of those events. This was the training ground for people who wanted to get into the roping events of professional rodeo. It's more difficult to break into roping because of the heavy expense of trailering a trained rope horse around the rodeo circuit. Some of the best ropers in the country have never competed outside their own local area. This is due, in part, to the fact that calf roping and team roping are part of the daily routine on cattle ranches, whereas the riding events are purely for competition and have no day-to-day counterpart. So, it's possible for ropers to find plenty of competition close to home, while bronc riders and bull riders need to be on the circuit just to compete.

Twelve riders signed up for the calf roping. Most of them were happy about the turn out. It made for a bigger purse. At eighty-four dollars it wasn't bad for fourteen or so seconds of work. Bard, Dave, and Adam were all within a second of each other, but Adam took the prize at thirteen point eight seconds.

In the team roping, there were only six entries, since the Grants, a father and son team, hadn't shown up. The competition wasn't particularly stiff, and Bob Gage and Winchester Davis walked away with it at an unspectacular time of twenty-one seconds. Most of the boys were frustrated about it, and promised to have another go-round later on.

To no one's surprise, Louise and Copper ran the barrels in a sizzling fifteen point eight seconds. Angie Tisch came in second with sixteen point three and got forty percent of the pot. The only reason for even having second place was so that someone besides Louise would have a chance of winning something. Otherwise, nobody else would enter.

Tommie Worth drew the second-to-last calf out of six entries. Louise was hoping he would get to go sooner and not have a chance to sit around nervous for so long. He wanted to get mounted up on Ferdinand the moment the event started. She got out a pencil and wrote on the back of a deposit slip, "Get your rope and keep practicing on that bucket. Ferd will get nervous if you get on him now. I'll stay here until they call for you." It was a lie, because it was she that was nervous- not Ferd.

Bob walked up just then and said, "Still warming up huh?" Tommie never looked up, but kept on throwing. "I just hope we can get him to relax. Do you have some string?"

"Yeah, I've got a piece in my pocket." Louise answered.

By the time Tommie's calf came up, Jeff had posted the fastest time at twelve seconds. Louise gave Tommie a boost up in the saddle. Bob looped the string around the horn and tied the end of it to Tommie's rope. Louise was saying, "Don't throw 'til he gets up close. Up close, ok?" Tommie nodded.

Ferd walked calmly into the arena like it was his own barnyard. He walked into the box, turned and crouched against the back of the box. The barrier was hooked and the gate man looked at Tommie. The boy took a deep breath and nodded his head. Tommie held the reins back until the calf cleared the chute, then released. They were sixty feet back, but Ferd closed the gap quickly. The calf's tail was even with Ferd's neck when Tommie threw. He pulled up and the big gelding sat back in a sliding stop. But the calf was still jumping and pulling at the rope. The string didn't break. Bob was over the fence in a second, followed by Win and Louise. Bob threw the calf and Win held him down. Louise took Ferd by the bridle and led him up and Win took the rope from his neck. Tommie calmly coiled up his rope, but they could see he was fighting back tears. Louise was enraged.

"How the hell did you tie that on there, Bob?"

"I just tied the damn thing on there. What the hell kind of string was that?"

"It was just string. You tied it on there, you know what it looked like!"

"It's supposed to be kite string!"

Win put his arm around Louise's shoulder. "All right, all right, you two. Just calm down. Let's see what the other guys want to do."

A small conference took place. They decided to split the pot between Jeff and Tommie. When they handed Tommie the fifteen dollars, he set his jaw and shook his head. He wouldn't take it. Louise put her hand on his shoulder.

"Tommie, I'm sorry, it's my fault. So you take half and Jeff gets half. Ok?"

Tommie shook his head again. He pointed to Jeff. Louise sighed, "Ok, tell you what, you and Jeff go again. Run it off. Is that ok with the rest of you guys?" They all agreed. Tommie nodded.

This time Louise tied the string on herself. Kite string. No more foul-ups. Tommie drew first. He didn't get off quite as good as before, but he hung in until he was close and threw. This time, the string broke. They flagged him in twelve point five seconds. Not a bad time. Now it was the older boy's turn. He was scorching. He got his flag in twelve seconds flat. Tommie didn't get upset. He ran up to Jeff and shook his hand.

Jeff asked, "We're still buddies?"

Tommie whispered, "Buddies." Nearly everyone came over and shook Tommie's hand. Dave Clayhorn told Bob he'd never seen such spunk in a kid before.

After that they had another round of calf roping. This time it was Bard who was in luck. His big white gelding scored the calf like it should be done. The calf jumped with him and was hard to flank, but he got it down and tied in fourteen seconds. It was good enough to take the purse.

By that time the Grants had shown up. Bob and Win were glad they did. It might be another ten dollars if they could get their magic to work. There were seven entries. A seventy dollar purse. Ty Lester was looking for Tommie. He found him by the timer's table. "Tommie, have you ever heeled?"

Tommie didn't catch it. Ty stooped down and wrote with his finger in the dirt, "Heeler?"

Tommie nodded and held up two fingers. "You've done it twice? Well, what the hell, want to heel for me?" Ty pointed at himself and Tommie. Tommie gave him the ok sign."

"Wait here." Ty said before he ran off to find Bob. He found him out by the trailers. "Say, Bob, could I talk you into letting me use Buck and Ferd? I want to get in this pot."

Bob said, "I guess I could. Got a heeler?"

Ty grinned, "Yeah, Tommie's gonna do it."

"Why not," Bob said, "he'll get a kick out of it. I'll pay his entry."

"The hell you will! I'll pay it."

Bob started to answer, but Ty dashed off for the timer's table. There was really no rush because the Grants were still getting saddled up. Ty and Tommie drew the last steer. There were now eight entries. Bob and Win would go second, so there was plenty of time after they were finished to change horses and readjust stirrups. This time, Bob and Win came in with a respectable eighteen seconds and change. But the Grants outdid them and put in a lightning fast time of sixteen point seven. The next three teams made tremendous efforts, but the time still stood. Ty and Tommie's steer had a hell of a big set of horns. Ty knew he would need a hell of a big loop.

He let out enough rope to make a loop four feet across, twirled it back over his hand and tucked it under his arm. He looked over at Tommie. The boy had his loop over his back shoulder and Ferdinand was in a crouch like an old tom cat. Ty knew that their only chance was a quick horn catch. But how far should he throw this monstrous loop? He nodded his head. When he saw the steer's rump, he whirled once and threw it as far as he could. It was too far! It shot way out in front of the steer. But, miraculously, the steer dropped his head down nearly to the ground and ran his horns right into the loop. Buck hit the brakes and spun around. Ty looked anxiously back over his shoulder. Ferd rolled back to his left and came up right behind the steer's left flank. Tommie was already twirling. Quickly he flipped his wrist and laid his loop on edge, right in front of the steer's hind legs. The steer walked stiff-legged into it and Tommie took up the slack. Ferd backed away until the rope was taut and the steer flopped over. The flag came down. A cheer went up around the arena. They knew the sixteen point seven had been beaten. Anxious seconds passed. Finally the timer called out, "Sixteen point three."

The cowboys were shouting and whistling. Tommie looked around. Suddenly he realized what had happened. He had won! He and Ty had beaten the Grants. This time, when they handed Tommie the money, he took it and grinned, as he stuck it in his shirt pocket. Everybody shook his hand again. Adam Hamber came walking up with a note and a piggin' string in his hand. Tommie read the note.

"This is the piggin' string I used when I won the calf roping at the National Western Stock Show. It's yours. When you get ready to start roping hard and fast, you can use this string and I'll help you learn. Your partner, Adam."

Opal was just ready to go out for a loaf of bread when the phone rang. "Hello."

"Hi, Opal, this is Louise."

"Is everything ok?"

"Couldn't be better. Say, there's a guy here who wants to talk to you."

"I assume you mean Tommie."

"No, the pope. Yes, I mean Tommie."

"Well, put him on."

"Ok, here he is."

"Hi, Mom. We...wuh...won. Won!"

73

Tommie handed the phone back to Louise. "Opal, you still there?"

"Yeah, I'm just, kind of... in shock. Did he say we won?"

"Yeah. He and Ty won the team roping. Ty roped the horns and Tommie caught the heels. The pot was forty-six dollars."

"It's incredible. I mean... he never talked to me on the phone before. Oh thanks, Louise, thanks so much! I don't know what to say. When will you be getting back?"

"We'll be leaving in about an hour. Here's Tommie again."

"Mom, not calf roping... team... roping." He handed the phone back to Louise. "Did you get that Opal?"

"Yeah, I got it. Just tell him how proud of him I am."

"Ok, we'll be seeing you when we get back."

"Ok, bye."

"Tommie, your mom's the proudest mom in the whole world."

Ty was sitting on the tailgate of the pickup talking to Louise. "See, from where I stand right now, what I'd like to do is get to be the horseback connection for a network. You know, like the ABC Wide World of Rodeo Sports, or the Cowboy ESPN."

"Like a roving commentator?"

"Have the standings of all the leading competitors in the PRCA."

"You'd know more about it than Howard Cosell."

"And a darn sight better looking."

"And can throw a great horn loop." Just then Bob Gage walked up.

"Well, Sis, what would you think if I was gone few days the first part of August?"

"Hey, I already told you, you should go. Did you think I changed my mind? Read my lips."

"See what I mean, Ty?" Bob said, "See what a smart-ass I have to put up with?"

"I wouldn't touch that line with a ten-foot pole," said Ty.

"You're just bragging," Louise said. "Bob, we're about ready to head back. Opal's dying to see Tommie."

"Ok," Bob said, "I'll see you when we get back."

Ty had to get a dozen or more color shots of Tommie and himself before the Fishers could load up and head for home. When he was satisfied he had some good images, he took down the address of Worth's cleaners, and told Louise he would send some pictures as soon as they were processed. By the time they had dropped Tommie off at his mom's place and gotten back to the Gage ranch it was after sundown. Bob was already home.

"I hope to hell he's got sense enough to get supper started," Louise hoped out loud. She led Copper into his stall and poured him some grain. She thanked Bill and Sonja for helping her out.

Sonja laughed, "Oh, Louise, we had the most fun we'd had in ages."

Bill said, "It wouldn't have been the same if you hadn't come along. What a weekend!"

Bob came out of the house before they could pull away. Sonja grinned, "Well, Bob, did you or didn't you?"

"Did I what?"

Louise chuckled, "Get supper started."

"I only made enough for me. You're going on a diet. Oh, listen, there's a phone call for you."

"From?" Louise asked.

"Oh, let's see… Randy… or Andy… or…"

Louise ran for the house. "See you guys!" she said over her shoulder.

Bob said goodbye to the Fishers and thanked them again. As they pulled away, Bob couldn't help musing over the way his sister had come to life the last few weeks. Ever since the city kid had shown up on their doorstep she seemed so much friskier. The way she'd taken charge of things while they were branding; the way she'd made friends with the vet and his wife; the way she'd gotten Tommie to get out and really try; she just seemed to be much more alive.

If it was love, maybe love was what more people needed. But if it *was* love, what a hopeless case it was. A guy like that could never get used to life out here. Maybe Louise would go with him. Then what? Bob shook his head. No, no. Too many ifs, buts, and maybes. He couldn't start dreading the future 'til it got there. He had to hope for the best but be ready for second best. As he walked in the kitchen, Louise was still talking.

"Yeah, yeah, I'll tell him. He might be real interested. Ah, nah. He's ok. He'll be fine. Yeah. All right. Yeah, I miss you too. Well, you call me if you hear anything, ok? All right. Bye." Louise hung up. She stood there several minutes looking at the floor.

"Want a beer?" Bob asked.

"Yeah," Louise sat down at the table and stared at the salad and sandwiches Bob had fixed.

Finally Bob said, "Well?"

"What? Oh hell, Bob, I'm sorry, my mind's running away with me. Hey, you made supper, thanks brother!"

"Well, what did he say?"

"Oh, he's back in D.C. now. He found Stan and Susan and got their car back. They're doing fine. But now he doesn't know where his brother is."

"His brother?"

"Yeah, all this time. It's been three months since he's heard from him."

"Sounds bad. But I thought they had connections overseas."

"None of them have heard from Jake. He's trying to keep his spirits up, but he's started to fear for the worst."

"I guess he would. Just the waiting and not knowing could drive you nuts. Here I was feeling sorry for myself in case you'd run off with him, and there he is worse off than I am."

"Oh, Bob, I'm not gonna run off and leave you here. We don't know what's gonna happen, but I care more about you than that."

"Oh, I know. We shouldn't even worry about it. I just mean that we should be thankful for all we've got. What else did he have to say?"

"Oh, he wants to see if Win will to do some work for him."

"Oh, what kind of work?"

"Like wrought iron stuff for kitchens and what not."

"Oh, yeah, like those big rings with hooks on 'em like you see in magazines."

"Something like that."

"Well, good, what Win needs is more income. I'm heading for bed. I'm beat."

"Well, give me a hug before you go. Right now I feel really lucky I've got a brother, and a ranch, and home to live in."

Louise and Sandy didn't know what was going to happen. They both knew they wanted to stay together, but they didn't know how they were going to go about it.

It was a warm, dry, sunny day. There was a slight breeze blowing. The weeds along the fences stood so high it obscured the strands of barbwire. Nine different times in the preceding month, thunderclouds had rumbled across the Sand Hills, filling the ponds, drenching the hay still in windrows, making the buffalo grass long and green, and the wild flowers bloom. Bob, in his faded blue sixty-eight GMC pickup, rolled right on by the mailbox, down the exit ramp, and out onto the interstate, bound for Cheyenne. When they built the interstate, it was designed for efficiency of use; not necessarily for efficiency of construction. If they came to a hill, they cut through it, not over or around it. It was easy on the tires, easy on the fuel, easy on the suspension. It made driving easy, but it also made it easier for travelers to pass through the country without noticing the natural grandeur of the surroundings.

As Bob got closer and closer to Wyoming, the hill cuts became less frequent as the landscape became more horizontal. I-80 runs east and west across southern Wyoming. It is one of the windiest, driest, and more horizontal stretches of pavement in the whole world. It crosses the continental divide without even a noticeable change in elevation. It's little wonder that people have a negative attitude about the state of Wyoming if all they've seen of it was through a car window on I-80.

Louise had made Bob some sandwiches and a thermos of black coffee. He had always had a good appetite, and preferred home cooked food. When he drank, he usually drank beer. He didn't smoke, but he was known to chew scrap tobacco on occasion. He had eaten the sandwiches by the time he reached Cheyenne. He was drinking the last of the coffee when he turned off onto I-25, headed for the Colorado border.

He turned off the interstate by Wellington, and headed west toward the mountains. There was a blue-grey haze across the Front Range and the hot air above the pavement caused the peaks to undulate like a belly-dancer in the mid-day sun. A small rainbow appeared above the end of a huge sprinkler irrigation system. The sun was dipping close to the mountain tops as he turned off into Porter Mason's drive and headed north along the ridge road. The ridge had outcroppings of sandstone shale and was vegetated with yucca, rabbit brush, cactus, and assorted wild flowers and grasses. The North Fork ditch had an elevation of fifty-two hundred feet- well below the level of most of the ridge. Porter owned the ridge. He had moved into the ridge about ten years before; about two years after he bought it from Dexter Jackson. Dexter owned ten sections of land in the area and really had very little use for the ridge. Porter had dug a tunnel through the ridge from west to east and reinforced it with steel and concrete. Then he built a home inside the tunnel with glassed-in solaria at both ends. He drilled down through the ridge eighty feet before he struck water, but it was clear and nearly distilled. The center of the tunnel could be closed off from the ends, and remained fifty to seventy degrees the year round. The ends were lighted directly and with reflectors, and retained forty percent of sunlight as heat energy.

The woman who met Bob at the door was early middle-aged and plumpish.

"Well. Bob Gage! I can't believe it, I was just thinking about you a few minutes ago."

"Hi, Joan. Just came to town for a few days to learn about test tube cows."

"Porter left early with Gator this morning to go to Niwot. There were supposed to be some free building materials available, so Porter took the flat-bed truck and went down. He also had Jennifer with him. I had to go to the doctor today so he took her with him. You've never seen Jennifer, have you?"

"No, I haven't."

"Well, you know she was born with club feet, right?"

"Yes I did."

"She's three, now, and just had her second operation, so she has casts on both feet. It doesn't bother her much, she walks fine, but we get the most hysterical comments from people. This woman in the laundromat said, 'Did your legs get broken, Sweetie?' Jennifer says, 'No ma'am, I had an operation.' 'Oh, my, what did they operate on?' Jennifer says, 'On the operating table.' So the woman says, 'No, I mean, where did they operate?' Jennifer said, 'In the hospital.'"

Bob started laughing, and it was several minutes before he regained his breath.

"Anyway, I don't expect them back until dinnertime. Would you like to stay and have dinner with us?"

"That would be nice. I need to call some people and let them know what I'm doing. I'm supposed to meet them tonight."

"There's the phone."

Bob dialed Ty and Monty's number. A woman's voice said, "Hello."

"Hi, I'm Bob Gage."

"Hi, Bob, I'm Dusty, are you in town?"

"Yeah, just got here. I'm at a friend's place."

"Monty should be back soon. Ty won't be home until after six."

"Could you have one of them call me when they come in?"

"Sure, what's the number?"

Bob gave her the number, then said goodbye.

Joan said, "Bob, you look tired."

"Yeah, I am kinda tired. Up late last night, then driving out this morning."

"Why don't you take a nap on the sofa? I'll wake you when Porter gets back."

"Sounds like a good idea, I think I will."

Joan started getting dinner together while Bob laid back and closed his eyes. It wasn't long before he had fallen asleep. He dreamed he was at a cabin in a dark forest. There was a well outside the cabin with a wooden frame around it and a shingled roof over it. He was lowering a galvanized bucket into the well and then pulling it up again, full to the brim with cold clear water. After that bucketful, he fetched another, then another, then another. He kept lowering and raising the bucket again and again, but more water was needed. He began to hear laughter off in the distance. First it was faint; then it grew louder and louder as if someone were coming closer and closer, laughing as they came. He started waking up. The laughter was in the same room. Joan was on the phone. She would listen several moments, then break into uproarious laughter. The laughter would just subside for a few moments, then start again. Whoever was on the phone (he guessed it was Porter) had Joan in stitches by what he was saying. Bob became curious to know what it was. He knew it wasn't about him, surely by now Joan would have heard all the stories Porter had to tell about

Bob. When Joan finally hung up the phone, Bob said, "What was all that about?"

"Ha, ho, ho… hmm, ho, ho… hmm, ho, ho, ha. That was Porter. He's… ha, ha, ha, ho, um, oh. No, I can't tell you. Wait 'til Porter gets back… ho, ho… let him tell you. It's absolutely hysterical!"

"Sounds like it."

"He'll be back within an hour. Oh, ho, ho…" The phone rang again and Joan answered it. "Hello."

"Is Bob Gage there?"

"Yup, just a second. Bob."

"Hello."

"Hi, this Ty. When are you coming over?"

"Just waiting for this guy to get home so we can eat dinner. I'm kinda anxious for him to get here. I guess he has this incredibly funny story to tell me. I'll be over after that. I guess around eight."

"Eight o'clock? Ok, sounds good. Don't forget to let us in on the joke when you get here."

"Ok, I won't. Catch you later."

"Bye."

Joan was struggling to make a New England boiled dinner take on a tangible sensation by putting things like tarragon and rosemary into the pot. Bob was sharpening his knife and listening to Leo Kotke.

Porter and Gator showed up at 6:45 with Jennifer asleep over Porter's shoulder. After about six pounds of boiled beef, onions, carrots, potatoes and rosemary, Porter lit his pipe and started telling Bob about how they had left the ridge early Thursday.

Porter had a dog named Rupert that had the coloration of a Dalmatian, with the build of a Labrador. He was known to be a loyal pet, but somewhat eccentric. His stubbornness got to be, if anything, more habitual as he got older. He would very slowly and deliberately snap at anyone who tried to make a fool out of him in any way.

They had set out for Niwot at nine a.m. when the weather was balmy and the sky was clear. By the time they got to Niwot, it was downright sultry. A crew was

81

tearing down an old Spanish style building and they were discarding a lot of roof tiles and sandstone blocks. Porter and Gator had loaded as many roof tiles as they could on the truck, but had left a space for a small icebox that was being thrown out. There wasn't any way of tying the icebox in a standing position, so they laid it down and put Jennifer, with her four pounds of plaster, on top to weigh it down. Rupert insisted on sitting on the seat of the truck cab, which would have Gator sitting nearly on top of him, so instead, Gator stood on the running board so he could, at least, catch the breeze driving down the road.

Rupert's tongue was hanging out and he panted continuously in the heat. With everything loaded, they headed for home. Heading north on a county gravel road, they came to a stop at a railroad crossing. The rail bed was elevated and there was a large puddle of water from recent rains. As Porter pulled to a stop, Rupert just couldn't resist the temptation to jump out of the truck cab and go sit in the water. Gator yelled at him to get back in the truck, but Rupert ignored him and laid down in the puddle. Porter called him and Jennifer called him, but Rupert acted like he couldn't hear a thing and refused to budge form the puddle. Finally, Gator took off his boots and waded out into the puddle. He grasped Rupert firmly by the collar and started dragging him towards the truck. But Rupert was not about to give up easily. He bit Gator on the arm and when Gator let go of his collar, he walked back into the puddle and laid down. Gator was mad now. He started scooping up dirt clods from the road and flinging them in Rupert's direction. Most of them missed, but enough of them hit that Rupert's head and back were covered with mud. By this time there was so much yelling going on that a big herd of feeder cattle, in an adjacent field, got the idea they were being summoned for a feeding, and had gathered at the fence and started bawling and moaning. Gator soon had Rupert firmly in hand, again, and succeeded in getting him, wet and muddy, into to the cab of the truck. But all the pushing and pulling had caused the overloaded truck to bounce up and down, and the icebox on which Jennifer was sitting, began to teeter back and forth, with Jennifer bouncing up and down, and yelling at Rupert to stay in the truck. When Gator had Rupert in the cab, he slammed the door. But, when he jumped onto the running board, he slipped and fell off and landed on his back in the road. Rupert, eager to display his arrogance, jumped out the window and waded out into the puddle. By this time, a young woman in a VW had pulled up behind the truck. Porter had his arm out the window waving at her to go around. But the scene was too comical to miss, as she doubled over in hysterical laughter. Finally, after Gator got bit the second time, he and Porter managed to get Rupert back in the truck and Gator stood in front of the window so Rupert couldn't escape and Porter got in on the driver's side. By this time the feeder cattle had become very loud and feisty and, as the truck and its passengers pulled away from the scene, began running along the fence after them, bawling as they went. The woman in the VW was, by then laughing uncontrollably and it was several minutes before she could collect herself and drive on down the road. Even Gator admitted later that the event was amusing, but he swore it would be a cold day in hell before he ever went anywhere with Rupert again.

Porter asked where Bob was going to be staying.

"It's a place just off the road, on the way up the canyon. It used to be a dairy operation."

Porter said, "Oh, yeah, that place belongs to a woman who owns a bunch of beauty parlors in Denver. She lets those kids live there just in return for taking care of an old crippled horse. Rumor has it that there's been three or four kids who've made it through college just because of that old horse."

Gator said, "Why, hell, he might have died years ago and that's a stuffed horse standin' out there by the river and the kids can't let on to the old lady that he's dead or they'd have to drop out of school."

It was starting to get dark as Bob climbed in his pickup and headed off for Ty and Monty's. He thought he might ask them about the mortal condition of the old horse when he got there, but he wasn't sure if he could do it with a straight face. As he drove up US 287, he couldn't help but admire the surroundings. Sandstone and granite cliffs with cottonwoods and spruce juxtaposed at runoff level. No wonder so many people were trying to make a living in the area. It was attractive to him too; but he had the Sand Hills.

83

Ty and Monty's place was a low structure with basically three rooms, end-to-end. The rest room was out back. There was running water, but no one had ever gone to the trouble of installing a septic tank.

Dusty had dark brown hair and freckles. She wore jeans and a fitted western shirt. Her parents owned a clothing store in Glenwood Springs. She was majoring in botany and she loved horses. Bob was barely in the door when they handed him a beer and told him to "Pull your boots off and sit on the sofa." They wanted to hear Porter's story first thing. Bob tried his best to capture the humor of the event, but he just couldn't quite get it across the way it should be done. But the three young people enjoyed it anyway.

"Well, Bob, what's on your agenda for the weekend? Reason I ask is that Nolan and the Night Riders are playing at the Arapaho Lodge up the canyon."

"I think I've heard of them, kind of Bob Wills style music?"

"Them's the ones."

"Sounds like fun, but I don't have a date,"

"Don't need one," Ty said, "There'll be a whole bunch of un-branded heifers runnin' around."

"Beef heifers," Monty asked, "or dairy heifers?"

"Which kind am I, Monty?" Dusty asked.

"Uh, the good kind."

"Bet your ass I am. But which kind am I?"

"Any kind you want." Monty replied.

"I think you better quit while you're ahead, 'ol buddy." Ty said.

"I think you're right," Monty replied.

The Beef Breeders Conference started at 9:00 AM with registration and introductions. It went on for two hours and then broke for lunch. The afternoon session started at 1:00 PM and lasted until 4:30. Bob wasn't used to sitting in one place for so long. It reminded him of visiting the bank, which had always had a negative connotation to it. It was a large amphitheater type classroom with upholstered seats and electric blackboards. Most of the conferees were middle-aged or older men, but there were a few women as well. The talks were interesting, but he wished they would concentrate more on what kind of money was involved in this research and development, along with the technical details. Saturday morning they would be going to the research station to get acquainted with the equipment and handling involved in the process.

When he got back to Ty and Monty's place it was just about 5:30, so they decided to go out and eat Mexican food. The Godinez family made food that was hard to beat, especially the green chili.

Bob wanted it to be his treat, but he knew the two student-cowboys would give him trouble about it. So he sneaked in a word with the waitress on his way back to the restroom, and got her to hand the check directly to him after they'd eaten. Ty and Monty knew they'd been aced out by age and experience, so they secretly plotted to pay the cover at the Arapahoe and each buy him a drink as well.

As they started up the canyon, it was still broad daylight. The transition from plains, to foothills, to mountains is very abrupt in Northern Colorado, and visually very striking. It was fun for Bob to sit back and watch the canyon walls as they wound in and out from daylight to dusk and back again. Thank God for daylight saving time. There are a lot of people who live the year round up in the steep, wooded hills. They seem to have a quality about them that sets them apart from all plains dwelling people. They find comfort and a measure of contentment to live in a dwelling that is tucked away in a pocket of a wrinkled planet, surrounded by trees and rock outcroppings. They take pride in knowing they can walk outside and urinate on the ground anytime they want.

Do hill people beget more hill people, or is it the hills themselves that somehow subtly make the people their own? Through the summer months, they scurry back and forth (which is up and down), between their homes and their occupations, exuberant in the roller coaster ride down the creek, winding and squealing around tight curves on narrow roads. When winter comes, those same roads become death traps as they become iced over for weeks on end without a thaw. The "season of the slip" brings frustration, cold, and slush. They fight back with chains and extra drive shafts; sand and salt; lug tires and studs; shovels and winches; engine heaters and ether; push blades and front-end loaders; screams and curses; the battle rages on. They're pushed to the limit of human endurance, cut and chafed; sodden and frost bitten; and covered in mud. They pretend not to mind. But they do. Just not enough to have it any other way. They'll endure it all as long as they can. One more time they'll spin and slide, lock in the hubs, crawl in the mud, roll rocks into holes, and spit out the grit. The hills have claimed them for their own and they'll never sleep easy anywhere else. In the Rockies, they're mountain men and mountain women. But there is something about them they share with hill people the world over. Is it a lust for altitude? Or is it the isolation, the privacy, that elusive kind of freedom that can't quite exist in more horizontal terrain? There are the 'staunch New Englanders' of the northeast, the people of 'Appalachia,' the 'hillbillies' of the Ozarks and Ouachitas, the 'high country freaks' of the Sierras, the 'Penitentes' of the Sangre de Christos, and the descendants of Crazy Horse who haunt the Black Hills. In the British Isles, they're the Scots and the Picts. In the Pyrenees, they're the Basques. In the Alps they're the Swiss- speaking three different languages but united, because they're Alpine people. The Himalayas have the Hunzas, the Sherpas, and the people of the Khyber Pass. Indochina has the Hmong. South America has the descendants of the Incas, barrel-chested and robust. Many of these mountaineer societies support themselves with plant products that are treasured by some and scorned by others.

Whether legal, illegal, or quasi-legal, they come under the classification of drugs- although some prefer to call them herbs. Tobacco, corn liquor, ginseng, coffee, cocaine, opium, tea, hemp, beer, wine, moonshine, sassafras - the list is long. And who knows what the Yeti and the Big Foot are doing up there. Whatever it is, they know how to keep it hidden.

"Well I cut me out a heifer from the bunch of pretty girls
and yanks her to the center to dance the dreamy whirls
laid her head upon my bosom in a lovin' sort of way
and we drifted into heaven as the band began to play

JAMES BARTON ADAMS

The Arapaho had quite a bit of floor space for a honky-tonk that perched on a canyon wall, and catered to self-professed rowdies newly come of age, more-or-less contemporaneously with their getting drunk along with life in general, while surrounded by vertical surfaces at high altitude. "You ain't been bombed 'til you've been bombed in the sky." commented a cowboy known as 'Hole Card.'

Bob had been feeling exhilarated ever since he got out of the car. It was the cool night air and the smell of the evergreens; it was the clear sky and the sound of running water. Monty and Dusty headed for the dance floor as soon as they got in the door. Bob walked to the bar and got a bottle of Budweiser. When he turned around he noticed Ty had found Elmo. Ty waved a hand at Bob. "Elmo, why don't you show Bob around this place. I see a chick I've been wanting to talk to for a long time. See you later."

Off the back of the dance floor, there was a big green porch that hung out over the river, with an apple tree growing out of the middle of it. Bob and Elmo were talking to some people dressed in western clothes and boots. One was a lawyer, two of them were roofers; there was a carpenter, and also a fire inspector. When asked, "What do you do Bob?" he replied, "I raise cattle."

"Oh, my god," the lawyer yelped, "A real one."

"That ain't no drugstore," said one of the roofers. Bob broke into good natured laughter and the whole group laughed along. About that time, Ty came walking up with three bottles of beer and a brown-eyed girl with long brown hair. He handed a bottle of beer each to Bob and Elmo.

Ty said, "Wanda, I want you to meet Bob Gage. You already know Elmo."

"Nice to meet you," Bob said, smiling.

"Do you dance?" she asked in reply.

"I've been known to." They headed to the dance floor, then linked in the traditional ballroom style and did a simple two-step, making a slow, clockwise rotation. She was a small, willowy girl but she didn't dress to hide her thinness; the jeans were snug around her thighs and hips like a leotard on a bell-bottom ballerina. Bob pressed his palm to the small of her back and felt the firm muscles along the spine flex and bend as she tip-toed, feather light, to the rhythm of the music. They stayed on the dance floor through the next number, then walked over to where Ty, Monty, and Dusty were sitting. Wanda excused herself and headed to the ladies room. Bob sat down at the table and sipped his beer.

"Thanks, Ty, I really enjoyed that."

"Oh, anytime old buddy, anytime. Actually, as soon as I said 'hello' she said, 'do you know that big dude who walked in behind you?' But what can I say? I've always believed it was them that do all the pickin' and choosin', anyway."

"Yeah," Monty said, "they're always going, 'Oh, I don't care. You decide.' Then, you decide, and they say, 'well not that.'"

Bob said, "I could never figure out why they always have to go to the bathroom together."

Dusty spoke up, "She went by herself!"

As the night wore on, the dance floor became full to capacity. Even the best swinging two-steppers had to be content with what they could do on four square feet. By the end of the last set, Ty was dancing with the girl singer of the band in front of the stage, while the audience clapped in time with the music. Bob and Wanda were sitting under the apple tree looking at the stars.

Wanda was saying, "I'm working at this nursing home for the time being, but I'm hoping to get on at this thoroughbred breeding stable the first of September."

"You like horses?"

"Doesn't everyone? Yeah, when I was a kid in Arvada, I use to volunteer to feed and exercise peoples' horses while they were out of town. I want to start with a colt, train it myself. To barrel race, that kind of stuff."

"You should meet my sister. She could just about write the book on barrel racing."

"Huh, what's her name?"

"Louise."

"Louise... Louise what?"

"Well, it's Denton now. Used to be Gage, same as mine."

"Louise Gage? You're kidding. Your sister is Louise Gage?"

Bob chuckled, "Yep. The same."

"God, I can't believe it. When she was on the circuit- if she showed up, you might as well hang it up and hope for second place."

"Yeah, that's about right. But what about your family?"

"Oh, the folks are retired. They live in Colorado Springs. I've only got one brother. He's an engineer."

"What kind?"

"Well, chemical actually, but right now he's working on a wind-charger that can be made from all salvage materials."

"Sounds interesting, I've been wanting to put in a wind charger but all the ones I've looked at are too damn expensive. Salvage parts- that sounds more my style. How can he make any money on something like that?"

"Well, he won't make much, that's true. It's just for his own self-satisfaction. Hey, Bob, why don't you come to Denver with me and meet him. You'd really like him. How long is this conference going to last?"

"All day tomorrow. Which reminds me, I've got to be at the bull farm at ten o'clock."

"Yeah, I've got to be up early myself. But how about Sunday?"

"Go to Denver? Sure, why not. I'd like that."

"Ok. Well, why don't you ride down the canyon with me and we can talk about it."

"All right. Let me tell my comrades what I'm doing and I'll be right with you."

Bob wove his way through the clumps of people on the dance floor. It looked like Ty was making a concerted effort to shake the hand of every band member. Bob figured that the kid did have what it takes to be a professional journalist, if not a politician. But what about this girl? He'd never met a woman like that, let alone one so young and so pretty, so open, so self-assured. Maybe she didn't realize how old he was. He decided he'd have to talk to her about it on the way back. He didn't want to- she made him feel so good inside. But if he didn't tell her, he'd feel like a rat. But a rat who somebody cared about.

"Say, Ty."

"Yeah, man."

"Uh, I'll ride back down with Wanda. So, I'll see you back at your place."

"Well, you old dog you! We'll leave the door unlocked."

"Ready, Bob?" Wanda was asking.

"You bet. Talk to you later Ty."

As they walked away, Bob said, "You know, he is a hell of a good man."

"Who, Ty?" Wanda said, "He's going to be a good all-around man."

Wanda drove a Toyota pickup with over-sized wheels and tires. As they climbed into the cab, she stuck a tape in the deck and started the engine. Emmylou was singing, "I'm just a poor wayfaring stranger... "

Bob said, "Man, that girl can sing, can't she?"

"Yeah, I like her a lot. And that band is no slouch either." Wanda kept the pickup hugging the center line while she rolled along at a good clip, just like an old pro.

"Well, how old is this brother of yours?" Bob asked. It seemed like a good way to bring up the subject of his own age.

"He'll be thirty soon."

"So, he's your big brother."

"No, little bro... oooh shit. I should've known."

Bob was puzzled. "What?"

Wanda asked, "How old do you think I am?"

"Oh, I don't know. I just thought... "

"That I was a kid? Shit, no. man. I'm thirty-five."

"Gee, I'm sorry. I just thought... "

"Hey, it's all right. Happens all the time. They want to see my I.D. every place I go. You must be about... forty?"

"Close. I'm forty-one."

"Well, are you disappointed?"

"Not a damn bit!"

"Well then, why don't you slide over and keep me company."

He slid over and did. He was feeling like King Robert when they rolled up in front of Ty's place. He slipped his other arm around her. He was afraid to squeeze too tight. She seemed so delicate. Looks can be so deceiving.

"Call me tomorrow, she said softly."

"What's the number?"

"W.L. Taylor, it's in the book."

"Ok." He slid across the seat and got out. "See you tomorrow," he said as he closed the door. He slept better that night than he had in years.

It was broad daylight when Bob opened his eyes. He was just about to hit the floor running when he looked at his watch and realized it was only eight o'clock. Still, he didn't feel like sleeping so he eased into yesterday's Levis and went to the kitchen. He filled the coffee pot and set it on the stove to perk, then walked out the back and took a leak in the lilac bushes. The landlady's old gelding was standing by the pasture fence eyeing him casually. A sorrel mare with a three month colt, who were Dusty's pride and joy, were a little farther away. They were all standing in a well-established meadow which was sub-irrigated by seepage from the creek and looked like a bumpy deep pile carpet.

"Don't look at me old buddy," Bob said. "What you got is what most of us dream about. A comfortable retirement, good food, mamas and babies, and no taxes to pay."

When Bob walked back inside, Dusty was peeling apart strips of bacon and laying them in a cast iron skillet.

"Sorry I woke you," he whispered.

"Oh, no," she murmured, "I was just lying there, but when I smelled the coffee, I just had to get up."

Bob poured himself a cup of coffee and sat down at the kitchen table. Moments later, Monty walked in.

"Shiiiit. What's going on? I was dreaming about something, but when that bacon hit my nose, I forgot what it was."

Dusty told him, "Well, start making some toast and maybe it'll wake up Ty."

"Oh, shit, he was still listening to Willie and Leon when I went to bed. He probably won't be up 'til noon. What are you up to for today, Bob?"

"We're out at the bull farm today. Gonna get down to the real nitty-gritty part of it."

"We've got plans for supper, if you'd care to join us. We're going to the Dragon Palace."

Dusty added, "Chinese palace and Mongolian barbecue."

"Mongolian what?"

"Barbecue." Monty explained. "I'd tell you about it but it would be more fun for you to see for yourself. But I guarantee you'll like it."

"Sounds all right to me." Bob said.

"Well, just meet us back here when you're done with the conference." Monty said.

"Good enough." Bob agreed. "I've got to run if I'm gonna make it on time. See you guys later."

Bob was duly impressed with the layout of the bull farm. Nearly every breed of cattle was represented and embryos of any of them were available. There was a lot of experimentation going on as these new techniques opened up new avenues of inquiry."

When they broke for lunch, Bob went to call Wanda. He remembered the name because it was a cross between Old Taylor and W.L. Weller. She answered on the second ring.

"Hello."

"Hi, it's Bob."

"Hi, Bob, What time is it?"

"About noon."

"Damn, time for lunch and I haven't had breakfast yet. So, what's up?"

"Want to get some lunch?"

"How much time have you got?"

"About forty-five minutes."

"Nah, skip it. What are you doing later?"

"Well, if you're interested, these guys I'm staying with want to go to some Mongolian Barbecue when I get back."

"Hey, great. That place is a real trip."

"Well, I'm finished around five o'clock."

"Ok, give me a call back when you get done."

"Ok, see you later."

"Bye."

The Mongolian Barbecue turned out to be both entertaining and tasty. It was an all-you-can-eat-for, which suited Bob just fine. The drinks came in an assortment of glasses with exotic names and an umbrella in each one. Monty was trying to get Ty to retell what had happened earlier in the day. Finally, after they'd eaten and were sipping on their drinks, Ty started.

"Well, I was checking around by phone, trying to find stories. See, I have this list of places I call that might have things going on with respect to agriculture, livestock, and so forth. Well I called this packing plant over in Greeley and asked if they had anything newsworthy. They told me there was this Holstein bull that was supposed to be slaughtered, but he knocked down the side of the chute and ran out into the parking lot and he was terrorizing the place- wreaking havoc. Dairy bulls can be quite nasty. Well they announced over the PA system for everybody to stay in their cars- and by the way, did anyone have a firearm. So this old boy, Scott Altenbach, had a two-seventy Winchester. Well, they told him, since it was his gun, to go ahead out there and try to drop the sucker. So, ol' Scotty sees the bull, lays his rifle across a fender, and shoots him in the neck- pretty as you please. They said this guy is from here in town, so I looked him up in the phone book and called him. I said, 'I understand you're the fellow that shot the loose bull over at the slaughterhouse.' He says, 'Yes that's me.' So I told him I wanted to write a little human interest story about it and he says, 'Sure, fine.' So I said, 'what brought you out to the slaughterhouse?' And he says, 'I was getting some blood for my vampire bats.' I said, 'Your what?' 'Yeah, I'm a grad student in zoology and I've got these vampire bats, and they need blood.' So I write this story and drop it off at the paper. A while later, the editor calls and says, 'What the hell are you up to, Ty?' I'm paying you to write serious news stories and we don't need somebody playing games with our readers. So I said, 'Boss, I'm telling it like it is.' He says, 'Oh sure, student shoots bull while getting blood for bats. What kind of crap is that?' The son-of-a-bitch thinks I'm jivin' him. So what the hell can I do?"

Monty said, "By god, we ought to drink to them vampire bats. Waitress, give us another round over here. We're gonna drink a toast to the vampire bats."

When the celebration of Ty's comical episode was winding down, Dusty suggested they all read their fortunes from the cookies, one at a time. Ty's read, 'You will always get what you want through your charm and personality.' Monty's read, 'You love Chinese food.' Dusty's read, 'Be careful to avoid getting involved in what you do not need.' Wanda's read, 'You'll meet an attractive stranger who will influence you greatly.' Bob's read, 'Do not place great importance in the opinions of others.'

The night was still young and the moon had just come up- rounded and yellow. Since Nolan and the Nightriders were playing at the Arapaho again, they headed up the canyon. Wanda asked Bob if he'd drive and he agreed. When they were on the north end of town, Wanda asked, "Bob, do you mind if I smoke a joint?"

"No, I don't mind at all."

"You want some?"

"No thanks. I've tried it, but I found that if I drank anything at all, it made me feel sick."

"Yeah, happens to a lot of people. Doesn't do that to me, but I do have to be careful about how much of each one I do, especially when I have to drive down a mountain road afterwards."

"I can imagine."

"Ever shoot pool?"

"Yeah, sometimes. I never was too good."

"Want to shoot a game when we get there?"

"Sure. But don't expect me to be good competition."

When they arrived at the Arapaho, Bob went to the bar for some beers while Wanda went to put quarters on the table. One table wasn't being used, so Wanda racked the balls. Bob came in and handed her a beer. "Would you like to break, Bob?"

"Love to." Bob hit the cue ball square into the middle of the nose ball. The balls scattered and ricocheted around. Two stripes and one solid went in and the cue ball bounced off the table and onto the floor. Bob picked it up and handed it to Wanda. She put it on the table and proceeded to run all the striped balls off the table. She tried to bank in the eight and missed. Bob dropped in two solid balls and scratched. A cowboy in a flowered shirt walked up and asked, "Mind if I challenge the table?"

Bob said, "No, go right ahead."

Wanda commented, "Damn, you're easy to please."

"Hey, it's all right," he said, "I'm not going anywhere."

Wanda put the eight in the side pocket and the flowered shirt cowboy put in his quarters. He lasted through four of his balls, then went down. The next guy up looked like Waylon Jennings, but not as old. He racked the balls and sat down next to Bob. He leaned over and said, "Unless somebody gets lucky, she'll be on the table all night."

Bob replied, "I can believe it. I just played her."

Waylon didn't even get a shot. As the eight ball rolled in, he said, "Shit," with a good natured grin."

The next man wanted to play doubles, so Wanda enlisted Bob's help, and asked their opponents if they wanted to play for a beer apiece. They agreed and Bob broke the rack, very much like he had before. As the night wore on, Bob lost track of how many games they played. By midnight, they still hadn't had to pay for any more beer. When, finally, she scratched on a bank shot, she sat down next to Bob. "Guess I'm getting tired," she said.

Bob said, "I'm really not so tired, but I sure could enjoy having you all to myself for a while."

Wanda grinned, "Yeah, I think there's something we haven't gotten around to yet."

Bob drove back. Wanda kept both hands wrapped around his right arm as if she was afraid that if she let go, he would disappear.

When Bob woke up the next morning, he was in bed alone. His neck and right shoulder were stiff from sleeping with his arm in an awkward position. He hadn't slept terribly well, but he wasn't accustomed to sleeping with another person. He could hear the sound of a percolator in the next room. He rolled over and looked at his watch. It was ten AM. He had a quick thought- what had happened last night seemed natural, it felt right. But he made a point to remember to get himself into a comfortable position before falling asleep.

Suddenly, there was the sound of guitars, mandolins, and a woman's voice.

"I met my darlin' in the spring time,

When all the flowers were in bloom.

And like the flowers our love blossomed,

We married in the month of June."

It was Emmylou Harris, but an album he hadn't heard. It was nice. He sat up and rubbed his shoulder. It wasn't bad, but it reminded him of something he didn't want to think about. Something inside of him was telling him, "You can't go through this again. You can't do this… again…what the hell? You can't do anything again. Each day is different." He pulled his underwear on and walked into the kitchen rubbing his sore shoulder. He looked for a couple of seconds at the thin little woman pouring coffee. She turned and looked at him, then walked over with outstretched arms. He lifted her off her feet and held her close with his face to her neck.

"You look worried, Bob. Are you worried?"

"Yes, I guess."

"About what?"

"I can't remember. I almost remembered, but you made me forget."

"Good! Whatever it is, forget it. Today is today."

"Our love was like a burning ember.

It warmed us as the cold winds blow,

We had sunshine in December

And grew our roses in the snow."

"I know that's Emmylou, but what album is that?" Bob wanted to know.

"Roses in the snow. It just came out. Do you like it?"

"It's great. That must be the Hot Band."

"That's the ones."

It was noon by the time they left Ft Collins. It was a cool, clear day with very little breeze. Wanda was driving and they were listening to Willie Nelson. Bob had a feeling that there were things he should talk to Wanda about, but he didn't know where to start. Then he realized that there wasn't really anything to talk about. What happened in the past was related to now, but it was distinct from now. He decided to just let this relationship happen, without assuming or expecting anything. Just let it happen. He began to feel more relaxed.

"So, what do you do at the nursing home?" he asked her.

"Practice nursing."

"Does that mean you're a nurse?"

"Yep, L.P.N."

"I thought that was a good skill to have."

"It is and it isn't. Back when I was a kid, nursing was one of the few professions available to women. But as an L.P.N., the hospitals expect you to take responsibility for the patient, but you're not in on any decisions being made. The wages they offer just aren't high enough to take on that kind of responsibility. At least at the nursing home, we don't have to take on that responsibility, and it pays just as well."

"What about R.N.s?"

"R.N.s get paid a lot better and to some doctors their input is welcomed. I've thought about going back and getting registered, but right now I feel like doing something else for a while and see how it works out."

"Well, I know you like horses. How do you feel about cows?"

"Cows? Well, cow is the first part of cowgirl, and cow-horse has a certain ring to it. I think, probably, if I got to ride a horse while I was fooling with cows, I could get right into it."

Bob nodded. He was a little surprised at himself for asking the question, but he was pleased with the answer she gave him.

Jim's place was ten miles east of Denver. It wasn't enough in the country to be rustic and did not benefit from the city's proximity, either. The site was chosen, Wanda explained, for no other reason than it was hellaciously windy. It was noticeably windy that day, judging from the activity of Jim's wind chargers. He had four poles, about the size of telephone poles, each equipped with blades. Two of his blades were mounted vertically and two were mounted horizontally. The only building was a one-story cinderblock cubicle. Jim was about six feet tall with a medium build and grey eyes. His hair was light brown and he didn't look much like Wanda.

"I'm happy to meet anybody who prompts my big sister to visit me." Jim declared. "How did you do that, Bob?"

"Oh, I don't know," Bob replied, we got to talking about families. Turns out we both came from a family with just two kids."

"His sister is Louise Gage." Wanda added.

"That's nice," Jim said, frowning slightly.

"You know, she won damn near every barrel race we saw for about three years."

"The one that never used a quirt?"

"That never used a quirt. Right!"

"Oh, that Louise Gage. Well", Jim said, "let me show you around. This area in the front of the building is my living area. It's my kitchen, bedroom, and living room. I've got conventional power in here except my lights can be run off my wind-chargers." Jim showed them into the back room.

Whirring and clattering sounds pervaded the area. "This is all wind power in here." There were at least two dozen clocks in the room. Some ticked, and some hummed. There were lights of all kinds- neon, fluorescent, incandescent, mercury vapor, grow-lights, flashing lights, lava lamps, LEDs and Christmas tree lights included. In the middle of the room was a large table with an electric train set up.

Jim threw a switch and the train began to move around the table. There was a stereo at one end of the room with both a turntable and a tape deck and large speakers in the corners. There were four different keyboard instruments near the stereo. There were several potted plants with lights directly above. There was a fifty gallon aquarium with tropical fish. It was equipped with an aerator, filter and lights. There was a TV, a home computer and various pieces of electronic equipment that Bob didn't recognize.

"How much of this stuff," Bob asked, "can you run at one time?"

Jim chuckled, "All of it. I'd turn it all on and show you, but it gets too noisy to stand. Take my word for it. The key, though, is that these are all low wattage devices, and for low wattage, you can get away with low voltage. The train draws the most current. Not because of the motor itself, but because of the load on the motor."

"Because it moves?" Bob asked.

"Exactly. Causes drag on the rotation."

Bob nodded, "Impressive, but how do you store the power?"

"Batteries," Jim replied, switching off the train, "Twelve volt automotive batteries. They're over here." Jim opened a metal door to a small room. The floor was covered with an assortment of batteries. "I'm using lead sulfate batteries because they're readily available. Some I picked up cheap from wrecking yards, some I bought new, but I'm trying to keep costs at a minimum. It's not so much what can be done, but how it can be done cheaply and easily."

"So all it is," Bob queried, "is automotive charging systems?"

"You got it," Jim replied. "Alternators and regulators. You catch on quick. Where'd you find this guy Wanda?"

"Picked him up in a bar. What of it?"

Jim and Bob both laughed. Bob said, "You realize, of course, that farmers and ranchers had wind powered electric generators a long time ago."

"Yes, I know. Then REA came along and the power was so cheap, people quit using them. There are still old Aeromotor rigs around that we could start using again."

Bob said, "But I don't see how many people could find this hard to understand."

"Oh, you'd be surprised," Jim returned, "the energy department wants me to write it up cookbook style, so the average guy knows, step-by-step, how to proceed. Actually, the hardest part is the tower and the blade, and bearings. It all depends on what you can get your hands on. I've used several different methods and they're all functional. Now a guy like you might have a tower available."

"Yes, I do. I have three I pump water with. Mighty handy, that wind."

"Well, we sailed across the ocean with it for centuries."

"So, are you going to do this cookbook thing?" Wanda asked.

Jim sighed, "I guess so. They'll pay me for it, so I might as well. Thing is, they want to tell the consumer to have their charging system checked by a licensed electrician."

Bob nodded, "Who won't know anything about it."

"Right," Jim agreed. "He's in more danger of falling off the tower than he is of the electricity. But, I don't think I want to be responsible, either way."

"Well," Bob asserted, "You've got me interested. I'm gonna get something going as soon as I get back home."

"All that wind going to waste, huh?" Wanda quipped.

"Where do you live, Bob?" Jim asked.

"Western Nebraska. Sand Hills."

"Ah, perfect," Jim smiled. "Good prevailing winds."

"Yeah, it's got the wind, all right." Bob agreed.

"Well, Nurse Taylor," Jim began, "I trust the two of you will be staying for dinner?"

"Damn right, Jimbo," Wanda announced. "You don't think I'd come visit you if you didn't feed me."

Bob chuckled, "Sounds like a rhetorical question to me. Let me borrow your keys, Wanda I'm going after some beer."

"Ok, get this turkey some Coors, he won't drink anything else."

Bob headed for the liquor store and Jim took a package of hamburger out of the freezer, and put a skillet on the stove. "He seems like a real nice man, Sis, how big is his spread?"

"He's got around three hundred head and enough land for them. I know you think he might get into financial trouble."

"I wasn't going to burst your bubble, but at least you know what the guy's up against."

"Jim, I work with people every day who are at the end of their rope, but that doesn't mean life is going out of style."

The hamburger sizzled as Jim dropped it in the skillet. Wanda went on. "I'm getting sick of seeing people use each other. Manipulating. Smiling while you can't see what their hands are doing. Stuffing toot up their nose at night, then slipping off before the sun comes up. Shit, I'm just as guilty of it as the rest of them. But it's not right. I want to love somebody. I want somebody to care about me- not what I do or who my parents are. Some of those old guys in the home love you just because you're there. And they're at peace with themselves." Her voice trailed off.

Jim put a lid on the skillet and took a head of lettuce and a tomato out of the refrigerator. "I care about you, Wanda. I didn't used to. I hated you because you got to do things I didn't."

Wanda laughed, "I used to hate you because you were a boy. I thought Mom and Dad liked you better."

Jim nodded, "Yeah, I hope you realize they really do care about you."

"Oh, I know. I just get sick and tired of them telling me how to run my life. Dammit, I'm in my thirties. If I haven't got it together now, I never will."

Jim chuckled. "Dad understands, and I think Mom is starting to. It's just that… well, imagine being that age and starting to think, 'my god, am I ever going to have any grandchildren?' That's what goes through her mind. Then it starts getting diverted off on me."

The sound of Wanda's pickup broke off the conversation. Wanda held the door open for Bob who came in with a twelve pack of Coors and a six pack of Bud. Jim was slicing up onions next to the sink. No one spoke as Bob set the beer down on the table.

"Haven't known me long enough to say very much about me, have you?" Bob said, grinning.

"Hell, no. Why'd you stay gone so long?" Wanda shot back.

"Cause that pickup of yours won't go any faster."

"Gimme a beer and keep quiet. I'm trying to tell my brother why I hate him."

Jim kept chopping at the onions. He wiped his right eye with his sleeve. "Thanks for the beer, Bob. You'll have to excuse her, she can't help it if she's spoiled."

Wanda was looking through drawers next to the sink. "Where's your grater Jim? This is going to take you all night."

"What's this stuff going to be, might I ask?" Bob questioned as he sat down on the end of the counter.

"Taco salad," Jim replied.

Wanda had found the grater and a chunk of longhorn cheese, and was creating a pile of stringy cheese next to where Bob was sitting. "So, Jim, what's happening with that girl you were telling me about?" Wanda inquired.

"She's a tall, slim, redhead. A geologist with some mining consultants. Haven't seen her lately. She likes to be outdoors- we've been to the mountains a couple of times. But most of the places she works are pretty desolate. Right now she's over on the western slope."

"Well, that must be nice country," Wanda remarked.

"Not necessarily. I mean, it's all pretty mountainous over there, but a lot of places aren't what you'd call picturesque."

"You mean, if it doesn't have trees on it, it's wasteland?"

"Oh, I don't know. I just haven't seen Kathy lately. She's been out in the field a lot this summer." Jim had filled a large salad bowl with lettuce, tomatoes, onions, and avocado slices. He drained his hamburger and dumped it in. Next he added a can of pinto beans, and then sprinkled Wanda's cheese over the top. Last to go was a large bag of Doritos before he tossed it all together with salad tongs. "All you have to do, Bob, is dump on however much hot sauce you want, and it's Taco Salad City." They all grabbed salad bowls and forks. Not a word was spoken for several minutes.

"You might not like my kind of country, Jim," Bob volunteered.

"I guess I've never seen it," Jim returned. "What's it like?"

"Have you seen Gunsmoke?"

"Yeah, a few times. You mean like where they're out in the country?"

"Yeah. Well, in a certain way, that's got a similarity to it. Only trees are along the creek bottom. The hills are grassy. Soil's real sandy?"

Wanda asked, "How the hell am I gonna find out if I like it?"

"I guess you'll have to come out and see it, won't you?" Bob said smiling.

"Or, you could send me some pictures."

"Which would you prefer?"

"Pictures can be deceiving."

"Or they can get lost in the mail."

"When can I see it?"

"Whenever you want."

"He's so damn agreeable, Jim." She looked over at Bob for a few seconds and said, "I'm going to come look at your damn sand hills. They'd have to be really bad, for me to not like 'em."

Bob, said, "I've met your brother. You need to meet my sister."

"I sure as hell need to meet your sister." Wanda retorted. "Let me get this straight, are you asking me to go with you when you drive back?"

Bob was nodding his head. "That's exactly what I'm asking."

Wanda didn't say anything for several seconds. Then she said, "Jim, you're a witness to this." Tears were welling up in her eyes.

Jim said, "Yes, I heard what he said. Anyone want any more salad?"

"I couldn't eat another bite said Bob. Thank you, Jim. That was excellent."

"Thank you, sir. Listen, I'll try to find some wind data on... where is it?"

"No Name."

"All right. How hard does the wind blow? We'll find out."

"Bob," asked Wanda, "Would you like to head out?"

"Yes, I would. Mr. Taylor, we'll be in touch. Thanks for everything."

When Bob and Wanda were back on the interstate, Wanda noticed she was almost out of gas. "Take a convenient exit, Bob, we have to get gas."

"Gotta get gas, maybe the taco salad will come through for us." Bob headed down the first off-ramp they came to. "Which way?"

"South, I guess, there's more population that direction." They were into an older residential area right away.

"Where to now?" Bob asked.

"Just keep going straight. We'll probably run into a convenience store pretty soon." A few minutes later, they still hadn't found anything. Wanda was getting a little anxious. "I'm sorry, Bob, I thought we'd find someplace by now." Just then the engine died for a second, then started again. Bob pulled over to the curb and shut of the ignition.

"Oh, well, it's no big deal. How far are we from Colfax," he asked.

"Not more than six blocks or so."

"Well, you wait here. I'll be back in a few minutes."

"No, wait, Bob. We can't do that."

'Why not?"

"This is the Five Points area. It's ethnic neighborhoods."

"So?"

"Well you can't just get out and walk, there's too much street crime around here."

"What do we do then?"

"We call for help. There's a tricycle on that porch over there, they probably have kids. Come on." They crossed the street and went to the door. Bob knocked. The curtains on the door moved and a black woman's face appeared.

"What you want?"

Wanda said, "We ran out of gas. Can we use your phone?"

"That your truck over there?"

"Yeah."

"You come on in, honey. Mister, you better stand here and keep an eye that truck. My grandkids has been here today and this place is a mess." Wanda followed the woman to the phone. "You gonna call a cab, honey?"

"Yeah."

"You better let me call you a cab. You call them white cab companies, they won't even come out here at night." Wanda waited while she called.

"Cecil? This Cleotha Johnson. Yeah, some folks need a cab over here. They run outa gas. Ok. Just fine. Bye." She hung up. "They be here pretty soon. Y'all just wait inside the door."

An aging Dodge taxi arrived inside of five minutes. Wanda was trying to give Cleotha five bucks. She finally succeeded when she said, "Get some ice cream for the grandkids."

The driver had brought along a gas can. It was about twenty minutes until they were on their way.

"I guess I was kind of naïve about those ethnic neighborhoods." Bob said finally.

"Well, chances are you might have been all right, but you can't take chances in an area like this. People who live here will be the first to tell you that. You even have to call the right cab company or they won't come."

"I'll know better if I ever get in a situation like that again. One thing still puzzles me, though."

"What's that?"

"If this is a black neighborhood, where are all these new Cadillacs they're supposed to be buying with their welfare checks?" I think I've seen about two since we left the interstate and they weren't new ones, by any means."

"I think it's because people see a black man driving a Caddy and assume he's on welfare and lives in Five Points, when he really lives in Park Hill, which is black, but not a ghetto, and he's got a good paying job."

"Yeah, I've kind of noticed that if there's any excuse for bigotry, a lot of people will milk it for all it's worth."

"Doesn't have to be much of an excuse, either. So you're still going back tomorrow?"

"Yeah, wish I could stay longer, but I've got to get back. Louise is probably about to chew nails as it is. When do you think you'll be able to come out?"

"Probably the weekend after next. I'll have to talk to the people running the nursing home. They'll flip out when I tell them I'm leaving. But I've got to give them some time to find somebody to replace me. Let me write down the address and phone number while I'm thinking about it." Never had a ten digit number seemed so important to her.

The phone ringing woke Jim on Monday morning. "Hello, this is Jim Taylor." He always answered the phone that way to avoid having to answer the question, "Is this James Taylor?"

"Jim, this is Ulrich Tinsley at Channel Eight News. Would you be interested in doing an interview about your research with the Department of Energy?"

"Sure, I'd be happy to. I'm free this afternoon as a matter of fact." He wasn't really excited about TV interviews and he made it a habit to get them scheduled for, and done, as quickly as possible. That way, he came off as being eager and willing and it gave him less time to sit around and worry about what he was going to say or how he was going to look.

"Would one thirty be ok?"

"Sounds good." Jim gave him directions.

The thing that bugged him the most was the breakdown in communication that occurred between his explanation of his equipment, and the journalist's understanding. To avoid this problem, he made it a point to start by saying, "What we have here is a wind-powered battery charger." Halfway through the interview he would repeat that statement, then, at the end of the interview he would say it again. Even then, some journalists would get the wrong idea. But, at least, they couldn't blame him for not being clear.

The reporter and his 'insta-cam' person showed up right on time. They were surprised to learn that wind powered generators were in widespread use back in the twenties, and that REA power, when it came in, was so cheap that the wind chargers were abandoned, even though they still functioned perfectly. They didn't seem to take much notice of the fact that alternators, which came into widespread use much later, were a lot more efficient. He took a good deal of time explaining what difference there was between low wattage and high wattage appliances and what precautions had to be taken when working with automotive batteries. The closing comments of the interview were made with Ulrich Tinsley and Jim, standing outdoors, with Jim's wind chargers in the background.

The interview over, Jim opened a beer that Bob and Wanda had left, and started going through his mail. The phone rang. "Hello, this is Jim Taylor."

"Hello Jim, this is Catherine of Aragon."

"Sorry, C.A., you can't have any more Tootsie Rolls, the peasants are starving already."

"Huh, huh. What are you up to?"

"Oh, just rearranging my brain cells. I thought you weren't going to be back until Wednesday."

"We hit gas a lot sooner than we'd expected."

"So, is it now 'Kathleen Kendall, famed geologist who has gas unexpectedly'?"

"Hit gas, Jim, hit gas."

"Oh, ok. Say, I'm going to be on TV tonight. Ten o'clock news, Channel eight."

"Do I get to come over and watch it with you, or do I have to watch it at home alone?"

"You're cordially invited. How long will you be in town?"

"I'm off for the rest of the week. Friday, I'm leaving for New Mexico to do field studies for oil shale."

"Well, stop off and get a bottle of champagne on the way over. We'll toast your gas discovery."

"Ok, see you in a bit. Bye."

Jim hung up. It was kind of ironic. He was a chemical engineer. Kathy was a geologist, whose favorite work was studying rock formations. Both of them were trying to find energy sources. Energy. Proceeding towards entropy. The flaming star throwing it outwards. The atmosphere soaking it up as the planet turns slowly on the spit. And we, Man- the divine spin-off. Trying to understand it all. Willing to dig into the dark spaces of our own fuse box to find answers. Ironic or enigmatic? Is 'why' even relevant? He grabbed his telephone again and called the office of the consulting company where he worked.

"Analycon, this is Vicky."

"Hi, this is Jim Taylor."

"Yes, Jim."

"Try to leave me open for a couple of days if you can. If something comes in, let Doug take it and if he needs help, he can call, or schedule it for later.

Of course, if there's a need to, you can page me."

"Ok, Jim, I think we can manage. Going camping?"

"Oh, maybe. My girlfriend's in town and I need a break so we can spend some time together."

"Sounds familiar. Ok, have a good one."

"Bye."

Jim walked over to his bookshelf and got out his atlas. He looked up No Name, Nebraska, and got its location. He went back to his computer terminal and called up data storage on wind velocities. He looked up in his data for some surrounding areas. There was too much discrepancy for him to get a reliable estimate. He turned the machine off. "Well, Bob, ol' buddy, looks like you get to be the first one to collect wind data in the No Name area."

It was almost six o'clock when he heard Kathy's 280-Z come roaring up the driveway. She had a fondness for the sound of a four cylinder engine and her exhaust system was set up so that the engine was clearly audible. Jim met her at the door. "Oh, it's you. When I heard that roar, I thought it must be a grizzly bear coming after me."

"It was, I made him sit in the car for acting like a spoiled brat. So what's happening?"

"Oh, Wanda was here yesterday. I think she's fallen in love."

"What, again?"

"Yeah, I have a feeling it may be different this time."

"Different, huh?"

"Yeah. For one thing, he's older than she is."

"That's a switch."

"And, he owns about sixteen sections of land."

"Wheeeoo. Well, who knows?" Say, I came up with an idea a couple of days ago for something you might be able to use. You know, wind power."

"Lay it on me."

"Well, suppose you had an air pump you could power off of a windmill."

"Yeah, that would work."

"Then, you could have it pump up an air tank."

109

"Hmm, it would need a safety valve, but that wouldn't be too hard to do. As a matter of fact, that would work a lot better than electric power, because of the torque it would have."

"But remember, it was my idea."

"Well, sure. Although it may very well have been done before."

"So, what's your schedule for the near future?"

"Well, I told the boss that I needed a few days off for some R and R."

"Great, what did you have in mind?"

Jim hesitated for a second or two. It sounded like one of her loaded questions, but he wasn't sure. "Why don't we go out and get something to eat, and we can sit around and discuss it?"

"Sounds like a good plan. But first we have to decide what we're going to eat."

Again he felt a distinct undercurrent beneath her comment. He groped for an idea with leverage to it. Finally he said, "Why don't you decide."

"Ok, the Briar Patch."

Jim loved to eat at the Briar Patch, but he didn't think she liked it very well. He felt like he was playing a chess game which he hadn't intended to play.

Kathy drove down the interstate with the abandon of a West Coast commuter, although she was from the mid-west. Jim trusted her driving, for no particular reason, and having the top down on a Monday night in eastern Colorado is a moment to be savored. He still didn't know what she was up to but he was playing it cool. He wasn't really worried, just curious. When they stopped for a traffic light, Kathy looked over at him with a smile. "You look like you want to say something."

"Do I?" he smiled back. "What do I look like I want to say?"

"Oh, I don't know. What did you have in mind?"

The light turned green and Kathy roared off down Federal Boulevard. Jim was moving his mouth but wasn't audible over the noise of the traffic. Kathy laughed. When they were parked at the Briar Patch, Jim asked. "Ok, Kathy, I give up. What do you want me to say?"

Kathy laughed again. "Wait 'til we get inside. I think I have a good idea we can talk about."

110

"Hey, you're just full of good ideas today."

They got seated and were looking over the menus. Jim decided very quickly what he wanted and laid down the menu. Kathy wasn't as fond of fried rabbit as Jim was, and when the waiter arrived, she ordered catfish. Jim ordered his usual.

Kathy didn't need to be prodded into talking. "I've been thinking... it seems like there are so many couples who wind up splitting up and then afterwards they say, 'I wasn't getting to do what I wanted.' Doesn't it make sense that they should have known what they wanted to do to begin with? Or, if they did know, and still wanted the relationship, they should have been trying to work it out so that they both were getting, at least, what they wanted. Does that make sense?"

"Sure it does. But I'm not sure that I'm following what it is that you're getting at."

"I'll get there. I just wanted to make sure you understand what my basic premise is."

"I think I do. You're saying we should find out more about each other's likes or dislikes."

"Basically, yes. But keeping in mind that we have to consciously make an effort to see that the other one gets their fair share of choices."

"That seems simple enough."

"It's simple in concept, but maybe difficult to apply. So, is it a deal?"

"It's a deal. So, what do you want to do this week?"

"It's up to you. This is your turn to fly."

"You mean you're going to go along with anything I choose?"

"Oh, I may have some input, but the decision is yours this time. Next time it's my turn."

"All right. I'd like to go to the mountains and look at the aspens."

"Should we take the zee car?"

"Nah, let's take my Jeep. I know some logging roads that hardly anybody else knows."

They drank a bottle of wine with supper. White Chablis- it was his favorite.

111

Kathy sat back and drained her glass.

"So, what general areas are these logging roads in?"

"Some in Pike Forest, some in White River Forest. I know a bunch of them around South Park. I know some spots with fantastic views- the kind you see on postcards and placemats..."

"And calendars?"

"Right. I know what you're going to say, 'why don't we just look at the calendars?"

"I wasn't going to say that."

"Anyway, you'll like it."

"Oh, I know. I like all the things you like. I'm serious. But I also like more of a variety that you do."

"I like variety myself. I just like some varieties a whole lot more than other varieties."

"Gotta hand it to you, Jim, that was a real gem, J-I-M, of ambiguity."

"Heh, heh, heh... glad you liked it."

Kathy could always be counted on for some good natured ribbing. She wasn't the best looking woman he knew, by any means. She wasn't the best dressed either. She stood five feet, ten. Her limbs were long and thin, and freckled. Her shoulder-length hair was dark red and her eyes were brown. She was motivated and energetic, but it was her sense of humor he liked the best. After supper they went by her place and got everything she needed for the next couple of days. It wasn't a whole lot- most of it went in her backpack. She was rummaging in the hall closet.

"Wait a second, Jim, I need a hammer." She found it and attached it to her pack frame.

"What do you need that for?"

"Just like you taking along your binoculars. I need my rock hammer in case I want to look inside something."

"But it's work isn't it?"

"Not really. At work, I'm looking for fossil fuel. This is more for enjoyment."

When they got back to Jim's place they loaded up the Jeep. They had everything ready to go so that when they got up the next morning, they could be on the road right away.

They were off right at sunrise Tuesday morning. By the time the morning rush hour was underway, they were on their way up Turkey Creek, headed for Kenosha Pass. Rising in altitude very rapidly, a sped-up progression of the seasons appeared right in front of their eyes. As they moved up the hog back, they saw cottonwoods along the arroyos. In Spanish the cottonwood is an Alamo. A trail along them is an Alameda. The leaves were mostly green with a few yellow ones here and there. Crawling on up through the canyon, they became yellower and yellower. Eventually they would reach aspens that were bare of leaves altogether.

By the time they reached nine thousand feet, it was 8:30 AM. "It's too early in the day to be so high." Kathy quipped. Kathy had a tendency to pay more attention to rocks than to trees- to erosion than to water. Jim was aware of that, and he could tell she was making an effort to talk about the scenery without referring to 'condensing gases' and 'glacial moraines.' He had gone out to see this spectacle of the changing aspens many times. East coast people were inclined to comment that there was 'too much yellow, not enough red.' Maybe they just found it hard to believe that that much yellow was actually there. Jim always felt that sky blue and aspen gold had a value greater in scope than all the material wealth man had found in the Rocky Mountains.

They ate lunch in front of an abandoned mine shaft in Pike National Forest. The view, even a New Englander would agree, was spectacular. They were looking into a cluster of mountains that represented the biggest chunk of over ten thousand foot real estate in the Rockies. The peaks were barren, blue-grey, granite. The slopes were deep green and brilliant yellow. The only signs of civilization were the Jeep, Jim and Kathy, the mine shaft opening, and one jet trail across the sky. Jim broke the silence.

"Did you ever have an experience where you were caught in the middle of a desperate situation and you had no one to look to for help except yourself?"

"I don't know," replied Kathy, "like what?"

"Well, one time I was deer-hunting. I was alone. I only had the weekend.

I drove up Friday night. I was way back above this meadow, which was a natural feeding area. There was snow forecast for Saturday, but what the heck, I'd camped in snow before. I had some new high-top hiking boots, which I had waterproofed, and a waterproof cover for my sleeping bag. I left the Jeep off the side of the logging road and hiked in about a mile. I put my stuff under a big fir tree and built a fire in such a position that it wasn't under the tree boughs. I had some soup and some beef jerky, then I let the fire go out and crawled in my sleeping bag. I left my boots sitting between me and where the fire had been. Along about midnight I woke to a crackling, popping sound. I stuck my head out and saw a bright yellow fire just burning to beat hell. The fire had kept smoldering by the needle mat until it burned its way up under those boots. All that fresh mink oil on the boots had caught fire and there was nothing left of them. And to make matters worse it had started snowing already. I got the fire put out and went to sleep."

"I'm glad to hear you didn't panic," Kathy laughed.

"I didn't panic, but I didn't really know what I was going to do. The next morning, there was a foot of snow on the ground. There was a pair of rubber boots in the Jeep, but that was a mile away. First off, I put on all the socks I had-three pair. Then I dumped out all the granola I had in a big plastic bag and put the bag on over one foot. Then I took the stuff-bag to my sleeping bag and put it on over the other foot. It wasn't too easy walking back with all that snow. I kept slipping and falling, and it was hard to find my way because everything looked different. But I made it back without serious mishap." Kathy was chuckling.

"What's so funny?"

"Sorry babe, it's not you, it's just like that Grateful Dead song, "Lost my boots in transit, babe, a pile of smoking leather, nailed a retread to my feet and prayed for better weather..."

"Yeah, I did have an experience like that one time. I was down by the Conchos River in New Mexico. It was in April, I think. It was a place where the river follows a crack that was formed by a fault slipping. It's very narrow and has an incredible descent angle. Really sudden drop off. Anyway, I was walking up and down the edge of this thing and wishing I could get across so I could see what

114

the wall on my side looked like. Then I saw a place where this granite slab protruded out from the opposite side and the gap was very narrow. I walked out to the edge of the wall that I was standing on, and that rock slab on the other side was about six feet from me horizontally, and about eight feet down. So I jumped across easily, with room to spare. Everything was fine. I got some great pictures of the wall. Then I decided to head back. I walked and walked, way up one direction and back the other direction, but I couldn't find a way back across. I should have known; the wall on that side was all lower. That's the way the fault slipped. Finally I just started walking downstream. About a mile downstream the river came out of that crack and spread out so it was fordable. I took off my boots and rolled my pants up to my knees. Then I held my boots and my other stuff over my head and waded back across that stream."

"Was it cold?"

"Jesus, it was cold! My legs were blue and there was no feeling in my feet at all. I dried off as much as I could, then put my socks and boots back on. By that time it was pitch dark and I still had to find my way a mile back uphill to my car. There was no problem with being lost- I knew where it was- it was just trying to find my way and hoping I didn't walk off an overhang."

"Which is much worse than walking off a hangover."

"Much, much worse."

"So, you can see what I mean?"

"About what, being disoriented? No, out of...sorts, luck?"

"How about marooned?"

"Yeah, it's as good as any. It should be 'maroonee' or self-marooned. I got to hand it to you, Jim"

"How come?"

"This is a hell of a panorama. Beats the piss out of any postcard I ever saw."

"Glad you like it. Want to go for some more?"

"Like, how fast?"

"Oh, nice ride up the other side of the valley, then next stop we spend the night?"

"Sounds all right. Where is that going to be?"

"Foot of those hills over there."
"All…. right!"

Not long after they returned to Denver, Kathy left for New Mexico to survey for oil shale.

THE MIDDLE OF NOWHERE
CHAPTER VIII
NIGHT WIND AND MOONLIGHT

It was one of those truck stop cafes where you didn't have to look at the menu, because you already knew what you could get and that it wouldn't cost too much. The sign with the two foot Coca-Cola disks said, "Eva's Café. The front of the menu said "Eva's Place". The sign painted on the window said, "Eva's Diner." It lacked a turtle in a pirate hat, but it was real down home. Two diesel engines outside idled with a steady rattle. Three men sat at the counter, two more occupied a booth, and two men and a woman sat at a table. The waitress looked like she had worked there all her life and had never let any food go to waste. Everyone in the room was drinking coffee except the woman at the table and she was drinking tomato juice. The man sitting across the table was heavy set and had black hair growing out of every part of his body except for the top of his head, which was bald. He was Tom Smith. He was around forty years old. The other man was older, late fifties, face wrinkled and brown, lean build- generally healthy appearance. He was Howard Jackson. The woman was Kathy Kendall. Dr. Jackson was talking.

"But you see, Tom, I've been in this mining business for forty years…" The waitress broke the conversation when she put down a plate of bacon and eggs in front of him, oatmeal for Tom, and a short stack of pancakes and two fried eggs for Kathy.

"Kathy, where do you put it all, you got hollow legs or what?" Tom asked.

"No, Tom, an active person like me uses up a lot of high-energy phosphate bonds, and carbohydrates is where I get 'em."

Jack smiled, "Well, you keep up with me, ok, But you see Tom…"

"I know, you've been a geologist for forty years."

"I wasn't going to say that. I just think that by the time you work with the BLM land, you wind up spending so much time and money on their environmental impact studies, their leasing restrictions, all that bureaucracy, you might as well have just bought property from private owners and have been done with it."

"I know, Jack, that's really true. But you forget, the Interior Department is just as anxious as we are to get kerogen production going on BLM land. The whole

117

atmosphere is different. Well, in any case, that's not for us to worry about, we're in exploration, and the object is to get our reports as objective as possible. Trust me."

Jack's eyes squinted. "Oh, I know you're right. The only predictable thing in this is the unpredictability. Right, Kathy?"

"You guys worry about the business end of it, I'm just here to break rocks and breathe fresh air."

Jack smiled and thought, "I wish I could do just that."

The coffee was thin, as it usually is in the Southwest. The people were friendly but not outwardly so. Rock, lots of rock. All different kinds of rock. But the coffee is so thin you don't even bother with cream. Not the kind of coffee he liked. Pure dark roast from New Orleans or Baton Rouge. But he had gotten used to the coffee they drank across the rest of the country. Not bad. But couldn't they make it a little stronger?

"But, I still think," Kathy was saying, "that out there, somewhere in that quad to the northeast, there might be rubies."

"Possibly as big as half a grain." said Tom.

"Possibly, yes," said Kathy.

"Possibly as much as twenty tons of soil per ruby." Jack added.

"Well, they are gemstones," she replied. "One would expect the cost of production to be high, but did you ever find a pearl in an oyster?"

"Yes, a very small one," Jack replied, "my wife still has it. Which reminds me. I promised myself I wouldn't argue with a woman."

"About anything but geology?"

"Right. What were we talking about?"

"Oysters."

"Ok, then forget it."

Kathy was laughing. Tom began jerking back and forth in his chair as he nearly choked on a mouthful of coffee. As the sunlight came streaming in through the café's front window, Jack paid their bill while Kathy went out to pull the carry-all up to the door. She let the engine idle. Tom was filling their thermos jug with water. Well water in the Southwest came in a variety of flavors. Some is almost

118

distilled. There are several different mineral salts that can be present. Kathy was thinking about Jim, back in Denver. She had developed an attachment for him, but who knew what would happen? She had to get to know him better, but that was taking a long time the way things were going. Right now she was out doing field studies much of the time. It was work she enjoyed. The fresh air, the huge expanse of sky. The never-the-same cloud patterns. They could be one thin layer at one elevation, stretching for hundreds of miles. Other times they could come boiling up over the horizon, tumbling and swirling, climbing up into a grey-black desert thunderhead. Sometimes they let a sunbeam come pouring through a small hole so that a rainbow spreads out across the clouds. Then sunrises and sunsets. All the shades of red and blue the atmosphere could conjure up as it paints the arid landscape with giant brushstrokes. If she could just get Jim to understand, you have to get down close to this country. Don't look at too much at once. Let your gaze fix on one small area at a time and let your senses open up and take it all in. Sensations you can't find anywhere else. Branching cacti that only bloom every other year. Huge forests of trees from eight to ten feet high and twenty paces apart.

"Ok, let's go," said Jack. He and Tom looked at maps while Kathy drove. The four-by-four carry-all had a tendency to bounce and lurch on dirt roads as function outweighed comfort in the world of desert prospecting.

"She can dance a Cajun rhythm,
Jump like a Willys in four wheel drive... Kathy sang.
"What?" asked Tom.

A jackrabbit jumped into the road and quickly began to outdistance the carry-all on the dozer road. Tom let out an, "Oh, yeah," then looked at the map again.

They agreed that they should stay on the dozer road for another ten miles, then take off across country another three or four miles, taking a bearing on a distant hilltop. When they finally headed off the dozer road, they had to slow down to nearly a crawl. Map reading became almost impossible. Just staying in the seat was a problem. Kathy was thinking about how many hours these two men had spent riding in the front seat of a vehicle going to or from someplace such as this. Kathy pulled up to the edge of an arroyo. All three got out and left the engine idling.

Jack spoke, "Head down that way 'til you hit that low bank. Then angle down in and across 'til you're back in the sagebrush. Want me to drive?"

Kathy thought for a second, "No, I think I can handle it. Besides, I need the experience."

Kathy climbed back in the driver's seat and engaged the transfer case. As she let out the clutch, the vehicle crawled along 'til she headed it down into the draw, then she stepped on the gas. The vehicle spun and pulled through the sandy stream bed 'til they hit the solid surface of the far bank. Kathy neatly kept the right-side wheels on the solid ground until she picked up enough speed to pull the vehicle up the other side of the arroyo.

"Hey, good girl!" shouted Jack.

Kathy smiled. She had long ago given up trying to correct the speech habits of guys like Jack. He was such a gentleman. It would be a shame to try to perfect something that was already such a work of art. He was like what she imagined her father had been. He died when she was seven.

It had been a warm day, but cloudy and overcast. She was standing next to her Dad in the bottom of an arroyo, much like the one she had just driven through. The old Ford panel wagon was parked nearby. Her mother was up on the bank. There was the faint sound of thunder off to the east. Her Dad was bent over looking in the stream bed. There was a sound like the wind rushing through trees- but there were no trees. Suddenly he stood up. For a few seconds he stood perfectly still, then he grabbed Kathy by the shoulders. He took a few quick steps, then swung her up to the roof of the car. He stepped on the running board, then jumped to the roof beside her. He was yelling at his wife to come get Kathy. He stood and raised Kathy up over his head. She put her hands in her Mom's hands and was pulled up on the bank. With Kathy beside her, Ann reached down for Robert- but he was already standing in waist deep rushing water. She only touched his fingertips as he was pulled away by the current.

Kathy could never remember what happened in the next few days- or the next years. Only that her Mom cried a lot. Whenever Ann cried, it brought back the sound of that brown swirling water. She and Ann enjoyed a comfortable life after that, but she'd always had a longing to tell her Dad how much she loved him but never had a chance to say it.

"Now, let's go parallel with that ridge for a mile or so," Jack was saying, "and watch out for big rocks."

"And renegades," said Tom.

"And big snakes," said Kathy. The smell of sage wafted through the open windows as leaves and branches were crushed by the tires. Up ahead they saw a flash of white as a buck mule deer bounded from the path of the carry-all.

The work was slow as they had to take several thousand-foot distances to locate their ridge. Then they had to locate their test holes. Tom and Kathy did most of the walking, leaving Jack to run the theodolite and coordinate the whole project. Tom walked because he knew he needed to lose the twenty pounds of excess he had picked up since last Christmas. Kathy walked because she loved to. There was lots to see here if you looked with an educated eye. Lots to feel and time to think. The fiberglass stadia board was fairly light. The land of incredible sky shows like the Mogollon Mountains of Arizona that Badger Clark wrote about.

"Squawk." Kathy's walkie-talkie came to life. "Kathy, I can see your mouth moving, but I can't read lips."

"Just singing a little song, Jack."

"Well, sing your way over to the end of that hogback; I'll tell you when to stop."

"Squawk. Ok.

> "Way up high in the muggy-ones upon the mountain top,
> A lion picked a yearling's bones and licked his thankful chops.
> When on the picture who should ride, coming down the slope
> But high-chin Bob with sinful pride and maverick hungry rope."
> Charles Badger Clark

"Squawk. Ok, Kathy, right in there."

After one or two more distance shots, Jack waved Kathy in, then turned to get a fix on Tom, who had worked his way to the top of a rock formation. Kathy collapsed the telescoping stadia board and made her way back to the carry-all. She wore kletter shoes, as she usually did in the field. Rubber soled running shoes were her choice for comfort, but for working in the field, the protection of heavy leather sides and Vibram soles were indispensable. Tom and Jack both wore high topped hiking boots, which offered good protection, but she couldn't stand the constrained feeling around the ankles. She had been a distance runner since high school. Her height and lean build had given her an advantage over the other women athletes in Jefferson, Nebraska. From her sophomore year, when she was already over five nine, she dominated the mile in the three school city meet. In her junior year, she walked away with the district trophy, but an ankle injury kept her from competing in the state meet. Her senior year, she broke the district record and tied for the state record. The day after the district meet, the sports page in Jefferson read, 'Cantering Kate Breaks District Mile.' Below it read 'Central High's Kendall leads team to district championship.' The sports editor, Bob Hertz, admitted to inventing the 'Cantering Kate' moniker. He was an old friend of the family, and when the men's team had put in a lackluster performance, he needed something with pizazz to head the sports page. Kathy didn't mind the notoriety, but she could never understand why he picked 'Kate' instead of the name she went by. Anyway, from then on she was often called 'Kate' or 'Katie', especially around Jefferson.

She didn't run quite as fast a race in the state meet, but she still came away with the first place trophy. Combined with her academic record as an honor graduate, her mother had a lot to brag about, which she did with relish. As an only child, she and her mother were very close. But it got to be embarrassing at times when she became Mom's only topic of conversation at social gatherings. And, having the pale complexion of a redhead, her blushing became renowned.

When she entered the university, she was keeping her legs in shape, hoping to do well in inter-collegiate competition and maybe the Olympics. But those dreams were shattered when she suddenly became ill in mid-December and was diagnosed with mononucleosis. Recovering was a long, slow process. Even schoolwork was exhausting as she tried to stay off her feet and exert as little as possible. It was well into her sophomore year before she could even think about going back into training. By then, the science courses and other requirements had become very demanding, but she dug into the material with a combination of fascination and determination that impressed many of her professors.

So the track competition was quietly laid to rest; but she retired a champion, and the running shoes stayed.

The orientation completed, the crew bagged up their rods and instruments and headed back to Ojo Seco. Tom drove this time. The way back seemed bumpier than it was on the way in. A person has a tendency to feel like relaxing at the end of the day, but off-the-road travel doesn't allow for it, unless you're completely exhausted. All three felt relieved when they finally pulled back on the dozer road. With all its ruts and potholes, it seemed like a turnpike after bouncing through the sagebrush.

Tom let up on the gas. "Looks like somebody has engine trouble." A faded Chevy van was stopped on the road. As they approached, they could see a man looking under the hood.

"Need some help?" Tom called out. Ramon pulled his head out from under the hood.

"Yeah, pal, I think we need a jump."

"Oh, I think we can manage that. Got some cables?"

"Yeah man." In the back of the van, Reuben's hand clutched the pistol grip of the shotgun while Tom followed Ramon to the back of the van. When Ramon opened the door, Reuben pointed the shotgun directly at Tom.

"Don't move man."

Ramon pulled his pistol from under his shirttail and pointed it toward the window of the carry-all. "Get out you guys."

Kathy's stomach knotted. "Oh shit."

Jack began to shake slightly as he felt the adrenaline pump through his veins. He took Kathy by the wrist and gently pulled her out of the carry-all. Not until she felt the ground beneath her feet did she become totally aware of what was happening.

"Take it easy," Jack said softly, "we'll be ok, just move slowly." Kathy realized she was holding her breath and began to breathe slowly.

"What do they want?"

"I don't know," Jack replied, "we'll see."

Ramon motioned them to the back of the van. Tom was already inside and Jack and Kathy climbed in beside him.

"You ok?" Jack asked Tom.

"Yeah, I guess. What do they want?"

"Shut up!" barked Reuben, "Don't talk now."

There was a sheet metal partition between the front part of the van and back where they sat. There was a small window cut in the partition but it was covered with aluminum foil. The windows in the rear were also covered, from the outside.

"What are they saying?" Kathy asked.

"I don't know," Jack replied, "they're talking too fast."

"Shut up or I'll shoot!" Reuben said fiercely. He slammed the rear door. They heard a padlock being fastened. The van backed up and turned around. They were headed back to the highway. They heard the carryall start up and follow fairly close behind.

"They must want money," Jack said.

"Most likely," Tom agreed, "but how much?"

Jack shook his head. "Let's just stay quiet and concentrate."

"On what?" Kathy asked.

"On where we're going." Jack answered. She understood. She and Tom were sitting on opposite sides. Jack was leaning against the doors. It occurred to Kathy that it would be difficult to keep track of linear distance and direction at the same time. She leaned over to Jack.

"I'll keep track of direction, you keep track of distance. Ok?"

Jack leaned over toward Tom for a moment, then back to Kathy. "We'll keep track of direction, you concentration on distance."

"Got you."

> For races nurtured in the dark,
> How would your own begin-
> Could blaze be done in Cochineal,
> Or noon in Mazarin?

"Now cut that out." Kathy told herself, "No time for Emily Dickinson right now. Got to concentrate. Second gear, twenty seconds. High gear, maybe thirty." She felt heavy anxiety adding the numbers. Running score. Should be a piece of cake. She wished it were.

Ramon held back and let the distance between the two vehicles increase. The Chevy van would pass unnoticed on the highway. The oil company truck wouldn't. They couldn't afford to get stopped. Reuben was right about the land. If there were rubies out there, they rightfully belonged to their people. Nobody gets hurt. He hoped Reuben was right about that. Anyway, as soon as they got to Caballo Grande, Reuben was going over to talk to Rudy. Rudy could plan things out so they worked. He could speak better English than he or Reuben.

The van stopped at the highway and stood for a second or two. Ramon stayed back from the van and cut his lights. Reuben pulled out and turned right. Ramon turned his lights on and followed at a distance. "Mother of god, let me get down this copulating road and not be seen." For the space of about five minutes they were on the blacktop in high gear, then they turned off on another dirt road. Ramon had been out this way only a couple of times. There was a little hacienda, long abandoned, that sat on an old Spanish land grant.

Tom felt the van slow down and take a hard left turn. He figured on him and Jack making a fairly close estimate on the direction. The road seemed to be meandering a bit, as if it were following a stream bed. The general direction he knew was south, but with the frequent turns it was difficult to tell if they were angling off. If there were a stream bed, it might give them a clue as to their ultimate location. He began to sort out the possible motives of their two captors. Had they mistaken them for some other people? Was it a simple kidnapping" (Simple?) Were they crazed, sadistic killers? His instinct told him they weren't. But, what if he was wrong? If it came down to someone getting hurt, he knew he would have to place Kathy's safety before his or Jack's. That seemed certain. He was starting to feel a slight headache coming, and his rear was getting sore, but worst of all was the anxiety. What was going to happen?

Jack was trying to steel himself for a possible showdown with their two gun-toting companions. If they could somehow spring Kathy loose...he knew she was smart enough to take care of herself, and the girl could run like a damn deer. But the thought of either of those guns going off made him shudder.

They had been on the dirt road for about half an hour before they stopped.

The back door of the van was opened. It was late evening. Ramon and Reuben had both guns drawn. There was a small adobe house. Ramon held the door open and motioned them inside.

"Move!" he ordered. Tom, Jack, and Kathy entered. Kathy noticed there was a full moon on the horizon. She watched the two Hispanic men from the corner of her eye. The taller one seemed a bit nervous.

"What am I scared of?" she thought.

> "What could a pair of pale green pants,
> Be standing in the air for?"   Dr. Seuss

Reuben had them empty their pockets. "You guys are making a mistake," Tom started to protest. Reuben wouldn't let him finish.

"Don't talk."

"But what is it you want?"

"Think you know what we want."

"No, I don't know what you want."

"Just stay here. We talk later."

Ramon walked out to the van. He returned with a half-gallon wine bottle of water and a plastic bag which contained a few flour tortillas. He handed them to Tom. "How appropriate, bread and water."

"Shut up." Ramon said once again. The door was closed and padlocked. The three looked at each other. Jack sighed and sat down on the hard earth floor.

"Might as well relax for now, pass around the tortillas." They sat there in the increasing darkness munching on the bread. There were two windows. They were both covered, but there were a few cracks between the boards that let in the last few glimmers of sunlight. Kathy spoke.

"Hey, this floor is dark red."

"Oxblood," Jack replied.

"Yeah, oxblood, but what is it?"

"It's really oxblood. When they slaughter an animal, the spread the blood on the floor. When the blood dries, it bonds the sand grains together and forms a hard surface."

"I'll be damned," said Kathy.

In a few minutes they heard the van start up and drive away.

126

Tom got up and went to the window. He squinted through a crack. "The big guy's leaving. The little guy's sitting in the carry-all."

Jack spoke, "I don't think they're out to do us any harm or they would have already... but that doesn't mean they won't if their extortion scheme doesn't work out."

"But we can't just..." Kathy started. Jack held up his hand.

"What I'm thinking is, if we could catch the little guy off guard, one of us might be able to spring loose and go for help."

Tom looked at him, "Well, first off, where the hell are we? We went five miles on the blacktop, then turned south. We must have been following a stream because the road kept winding back and forth; but it was basically southeast. Kathy, how far have we come?"

"Near as I can figure, about thirty-five miles since we started."

Jack chuckled. "That sounds about right."

"What's so funny?" Tom asked.

"Any place as old as this shows up on the quad maps. It's the only building within fifty miles of here. I remember seeing it on the map the first time we went over the area. I couldn't remember how far it was from the quarter corner, but it's within two inches, maybe an inch and a half." Tom nodded.

"Oh, so if Kathy figured it to be thirty-five on the road, it must be... what? Fifteen to twenty-two."

"As the crow flies," said Jack, "to the township line." Kathy was looking at the floor in the impending gloom.

"Now wait a minute. Let's get one thing straight," said Kathy. "if anyone's going for help, it's going to be me." Jack smiled.

"If Kathy wants to go, that's fine with me."

Tom shook his head. "Damn, I'm outvoted before I even open my mouth. The next question is, how do we get out of here, up the chimney?"

"No," Jack replied, "the chimney's too narrow, even for someone like Kathy."

Kathy frowned. Jack went on, "Actually, I was thinking of chipping the window frame loose from the wall... if only we had a rock hammer."

"We've got this," Kathy grinned as she pulled a long, thin nail file out of her boot.

Jack cautiously suggested, "Tom's belt buckle...?"

"My Tommy Singer belt buckle? Christ yes, think how much the son-of-a-bitch will be worth after I dig myself out of captivity with it."

Jack stood up and stretched. "Kathy, keep an eye on that guy out there and let me have a go with that file."

Kathy handed the file to Jack who joined Tom at the window. Kathy watched through the cracks between the boards covering the west window.

"What's he doing, Kathy?" Jack asked.

"Just sitting there. Can't see if he's looking this way... too dark."

"Well keep an eye on him. Let us know if he does anything. Moon's coming up. You'll have some light to see by."

"That is if I make it out of here."

Tom said, "Now cut out that kind of talk. You're getting out, we'll take care of that. You take care of the rest."

"You're right," said Kathy through clinched teeth. "We know what we have to do and we're going to do it."

A four-by-four carry-all. One small middle-aged Chicano. Probably listening to the radio. The cab light came on. Ramon was getting out.

"Ok, gang, our man's getting out." The digging stopped. "Probably taking a leak."

"Well, what nerve, where is he?" Tom asked softly.

"Other side of the truck."

"Must be modest. Keep us posted K.K."

"Right, now he's coming back to this side. Hold it, Tom."

"I'm holding."

"Now he's getting in. He left the lights on, must be reading."

"Or looking at the pictures," Tom said.

Kathy said, "Ok, keep digging."

For the next half hour, all that could be heard was the scratching of metal on clay.

"How far have we gone?" Tom asked.

"Inch, maybe inch and a quarter." said Jack

"How much is there?" Kathy asked.

Tom said, "Maybe five more inches."

"Can we do it?" Jack asked.

"Right on." Tom replied.

Kathy let her gaze survey the surrounding country in the moonlight.

Pinyon and desert cedar. "It isn't desert," she thought, low density forest."
Jack wiped his brow on his sleeve.

"Ok, let's take a break."

"I need a drink of water," Tom sighed.

"Ok, but just a few swallows," said Jack. "Kathy's got to have enough to go twenty miles."

Kathy felt a chill starting in her feet, moving up her legs to her stomach, then up to her chest. She clamped her jaw. She was still watching Ramon. Her neck muscles tightened, then she told herself to relax. A soothing warmth spread down her neck to her shoulders, then to her hips. Her feet were still cold. She rose on her tip-toes several times 'til the warmth returned to her feet. She felt warmer, more relaxed. Twenty miles. She'd be out there all night- but alone. Alone, but safe. She'd be safe—No! Dammit! They were letting her make a clean break for it while they stayed behind to face… whatever… danger. Dammit, why hadn't she seen it before? Well, she'd show them, show them all! She'd make it to the highway by daylight. She'd get the sheriff and be headed back within an hour, and have those jerks in jail before lunch!

Jack and Tom were back at the window. As the moon climbed higher, the low vegetation became more distinct. Were there rattlesnakes out at night? Would they be startled by a moving animal and forget to rattle?

Tom puffed and whispered, "It's getting loose over here."

"It's getting loose here too," said Jack. "Let's take a breather and decide what we're going to do. Kathy, over here."

"Ok, guys, I think our guard is preoccupied right now."

After several minutes had gone by and the men had regained their breath, Jack spoke. "We've got to get this guy to the door, but not through it. His pupils will be restricted from the light so he won't be able to see in here. Kathy's got to be through the window and gone before he can make it to the window or around the house. Now, if he moves to the window we'll yell, 'down,' if he goes back out, we'll yell, 'out.' Either way, Kathy will have to be out of his line of sight and then run for the bushes. Fifty feet will be enough to spoil his effectiveness with that pea-shooter. Thank god the other guy took the shotgun."

"How much water can I take," Kathy asked.

"We'll each have a drink, then you take the rest. We won't be doing that much."

129

"Don't be so candid," said Tom.

Jack chuckled, "Let's see how we're going to work this." They tore strips of cloth from Kathy's shirttail, and with these they got the wine bottle tied across the back of Kathy's shoulders.

"Let's get that window as loose as we can," said Tom.

"Ok," said Kathy, let me and Jack work on that while Tom keeps an eye on the little guy."

Several minutes later, Ramon heard a thumping sound. He raised his head. He decided to go check it out. Quickly he got out and closed the carry-all door. He listened. No sound. He pulled the hammer back on the thirty-eight. A thumping sound came from the house. He walked over and laid his ear to the door. Nothing. He hit the door with his fist. "What's going on, man?"

"We have to take a leak," said Tom. A few seconds passed.

"Ok, only one by one, man." Ramon held the thirty-eight in his left hand while he slowly unlocked the door with his right. "Get your hands up." He waited a few seconds, then stood back as he removed the padlock. Then he aimed the gun at the door as he slowly pulled it back. Tom and Jack stood in the doorway with their hands up.

"Whop!" The empty window frame popped out as Kathy hit it with both fists and her head, then dived through the opening after it. Ramon backed away from the door with his gun still aimed at Jack and Tom.

"Out! Out!" yelled Tom and Jack. Kathy rolled to the left and onto her feet, moving to the north of the building. Then she dashed for the scrub trees.

Ramon was screaming, "Alto! Alto! Stop you bitch!" BOOM... CRACK! One shot echoed.

Kathy slipped and fell, then clawed her way to her feet, then slipped again. She got her feet under her again and started her stride. Her left elbow was numb from the impact. The pinyons were around her. A voice in her head said, "Kick. Kick one, kick two." Her eyes strained to watch the ground. Her legs moved in an easy rhythm. No more shots followed the first one. The pounding in her head started to subside. She was out! She was dancing, weaving her way smoothly through the pinyons. Kick... kick. They couldn't stop her now. Nobody could stop her now"

There was only the sound of her feet on the loose dirt. There were only basketball sized rocks and small cacti to avoid. At her smooth cadence, she could adjust for them off her trailing foot. The wine bottle bounced at an even tempo as it rode lightly between her shoulder blades. The cool night wind felt fresh and comforting, and the surrounding scrub trees were distant markers as she moved herself closer to her goal.

I lit out from Reno, I was trailed by twenty hounds
Didn't get to sleep last night 'til the morning came around
Set out running but I take my time
Friend of the devil is a friend of mine
If I get home before daylight
Just might get some sleep tonight...... Robert Hunter

Ramon stepped into the house. He spit on the floor. "Chingau! Chingau Madre!"

Tom backed up against the north wall, then he lowered himself into a sitting position. Jack soon followed suit. Ramon continued to curse, but otherwise showed no signs of being more aggressive, although, he kept the thirty-eight aimed in their direction.

Kathy's elbow was still painful and one knee was scraped and burning. She lined up the North Star with a distant hill top and tried to stay on that same bearing. The terrain was fairly hilly, so she had to do some climbing to stay on course. The climbs seemed to outweigh the descents. She had a habit of letting odd bits of poetry and song lyrics drift through her mind when it wasn't occupied with something else. Running was one of those times. She had a good memory and could summon up many hours of verse. Shakespeare, Wordsworth, and Kipling. William Cullen Bryant, and Emily Dickinson. Lots of those old guys and new ones. Leonard Cohen and Galway Kinnell; Walt Kelly and Dr. Seuss, and Hunter- colorful and robust.

"Got two reasons why I lie awake each lonely night
First one's named sweet Ann Marie- she's my heart's delight
Second one is prison, babe, with sheriffs on my trail
And if he catches up with me, I'll spend my life in jail... " Hunter

The moonlight gave the landscape an eerie, unreal appearance, but there was nothing unreal about the feeling in her lungs and the ache that was starting upwards from her ankles. They had started almost at dawn that morning and had spent a long day in the field. She stopped and took a drink of water. A few minutes to stand and breathe. She became aware of the smell of the pinyon and cedar. A light in the sky was moving- an aircraft. Far enough away that it was actually far ahead from where the sound was heard. She thought about how that was like life in general. Everything we know is from observing the past. The only thing in the present is consciousness. Her watch read nine-sixteen. It had already been two hours. How far had she come? She could only guess. Five, maybe six miles? She couldn't stand the feeling of no motion. Got to move. Crunch, crunch, crack- over a rock, little jump.

> "Who rides in pursuit of a border thief
> Sits not long at his meat.
> He's up and away from Fort Bukloh
> As fast as a bird can fly,
> 'Til he was aware of his father's mare
> In the gut of the Tongue o' Jagai.
> 'til he was aware of his father's mare
> With Kamal upon her back,
> And when he could spy the white of her eye
> He made the pistol crack... "   Rudyard Kipling

Pistol crack! The thought brought her a chill. Tom and Jack. She had heard only one shot, but that was small consolation. Some gun-toting jerk. Deep breaths. Kick, kick.

> "The dun he leaned against the bit
> And slugged his head above
> But the red mare played with the snaffle bars
> Like a maiden plays with a glove... "   Rudyard Kipling

Put this distance in the past.

Tom gave a sigh. "And to think, I was only worried about nuclear war."

"The hell you were," Jack shot back, "you worried about who would play in the World Series." It was as once noticeable that Ramon had given up telling them to shut up. Still, it was hard to relax.

133

Crunch, crunch... bump, bump. Kathy froze and shuddered. Jackrabbit. He had jumped out of the brush and bounded away ahead of her. She laughed. "Just what I need, a rabbit. Take off rabbit, I'm right behind you. It's you and me."

> "Bent my ear to hear the tune
> And closed my eyes to see
> When there were no strings to play
> You played to me
> In the book of Love's own dream
> Where all the print is blurred
> Where all the pages are my days
> And all my lines grow old."   Robert Hunter

The ankles were hurting a bit, but she was becoming less aware of them. Maybe going a bit too fast. Got to finish. No record to break, nothing to prove but go the distance. Put this in the past. Starting to climb again. Got to slow up and rest, deep breaths, sit down and rest the ankles. Take a swallow. Got to finish. A few more breaths. Up and walking. Damn the grade. Short bouncing steps, loose rock.

> "One step forward and two steps back
> That won't get you back to Buffalo... No!"   Robert Hunter

Crest of the hill. Stop to get another fix on the Pole Star. Shadows up ahead. Big arroyo. They'd thought the winding road was following a stream. Tangent line along the east edge, almost north-northwest. Middle of the line- clump of rocks. Could be water in that arroyo.

> "When I had no wings to fly-
> You flew to me... you flew to me.
> In the secret space of dreams
> Where I dreaming lay amazed
> When the secrets are all told
> And the petals all unfold..."   Robert Hunter

"When there was no dream of mine
You dreamed of me... you dreamed of me."

"We'll just have to play this by ear." was Jack's comment.

"Just like life in general," was Tom's reply. Off in the distance was the sound of an approaching vehicle. Whatever vehicle it was, it brought the possibility of disaster for Tom and Jack, and cause for alarm for Ramon. As the vehicle came closer, they could tell it was the Chevy van. A few minutes later, the van pulled up to the house. The lights shone in the open doorway. The driver's door opened and shut. The engine was still running when Reuben appeared in the doorway with the shotgun in his hand.

"Where's the woman?'

"Outside," Ramon told him.

"Outside where?"

"The house outside."

"How she got the house outside?"

"Through the window."

"Chingau!" screamed Reuben. He walked to the van and returned with a flashlight. He stood for a moment panning the light around in the bushes, then he started off in the direction of the arroyo. Ramon waited a moment, then backed out of the house. Holding the gun toward the house, he went to the driver's side of the van and turned off the headlights, but left the engine running. The battery was old and wouldn't hold a charge very well. By the time Ramon returned to the house, Jack and Tom had positioned themselves against the wall on opposite sides of the door. Tom had pushed the door back against the wall with one hand on the doorknob.

By the time Kathy reached the edge of the arroyo and found a place with a gradual enough slope to make it to the bottom, half an hour had passed. Quickly, she slid down on the loose dirt to the stream bed. By the time she had gone a quarter of a mile, she caught a glimpse of moonlight reflecting off a pool just ahead. The water didn't taste bad and she managed to get the water bottle about half full. She toyed with the idea of following the stream back to the highway, but then she thought about all the time she had already taken and headed back northeast to give herself the straightest shot to the safety of the highway. What if the first car that comes along is in on this little conspiracy? Like Ray Milland in Rosemary's Baby. The moon had dropped well into the western sky when she stopped to rest for the second time since she'd left the arroyo.

> "All I know is something like a bird within her sang
> All I know she sang a little while and then flew off
> Tell me all that you know,
> I'll show you—storm and rain."   Robert Hunter

The pain from her ankles had spread slowly upward through her shins and into her knees. She had to go on. Go on if it killed her. If she didn't, it surely would. But she was so tired that if she fell, she might not be able to get up again.

> "Laugh in sunshine, sing-
> Cry in the dark-
> Fly through the night...
> Don't cry now,
> Don't you cry-
> Dry your eyes on the wind...   Robert Hunter

Tears welled up in her eyes. She fought them back with teeth clinched. Her mother's face was smiling back at her. The moon hit the backbone along the western horizon. She stopped at the top of a hill and drank the rest of the water.

> "They've ridden the low moon out of the sky,
> Their hooves drum up the dawn.
> The dun he went like a wounded bull,
> The mare like a new roused fawn."   Rudyard Kipling

To Tom, it seemed like several minutes had elapsed from the time Ramon turned off the headlights, until he stood again in the doorway. The instant he got there, Tom and Jack grabbed him by the upper arms and threw him across

136

the room. Jack ran to the Chevy van. Tom held the knob with both hands and leaned back. Jack got behind the wheel and opened the passenger door. He made a tight circle and pulled up next to the door of the house. As soon as Tom had one hand on the door frame and one hand on the door, Jack spun the tires and they sped away down the hill. Jack could see Ramon for several seconds in the rear-view mirror. He held the thirty-eight in his hand, but he didn't fire. The van was his only means of transportation.

The stars were almost gone. Only Venus still twinkled in the southwestern sky, which was turning grey. Kathy was walking up the ascents, loping casually down the descents. It was almost like a dream now. Her destination was only a short distance ahead. Only the status of her two friends remained important, remained to be learned before exhaustion set in. She was almost to the top of a gently sloping hill, when she heard a faint humming sound. At the crest she saw the lights. Lights moving from right to left. She was so tired she could barely remember why she was there. But her pace quickened. Down the long slope. Taking little descending jumps, keeping her feet under her, but feeling relaxed and jubilant. A mild euphoria. There was a blue van parked at the bottom of the hill. The right front door opened and someone got out. Kathy froze in her tracks. Now he was waving his arms. "Oh, god no! He's waiting for me. But why would he be waving?" She couldn't figure it out, but she was too tired to resist, too tired to think. The man walked around the van and turned on the emergency flashers. It was then that she realized that this van was a darker blue, and newer than the other one. The man walked to the fence and waited with one foot on the bottom strand of barb wire. Kathy was walking now. The man crawled through the fence and came walking up with his hand out.
  "You must be Kathy Kendall," he said as he approached. Kathy nodded. He didn't seem like the dangerous type, so she shook his hand.
  "And you're?"
  "Sandy Rose. I was just…"
  "Whew… we were kidnapped…huff, huff…"
  "I know. I just got recruited by the sheriff's office. We were just starting out to look for you." Sandy held the wire strands apart so Kathy could crawl through the fence.

"That's nice of you, but what happened..."

"To Dr. Jackson and Mr. Smith? They're fine. They got in last night."

"Thank God!" Kathy threw an arm across Sandy's shoulders as they walked toward the van. She was considerably taller than he, but lighter. "But what happened?"

"I don't know for sure, but I know one thing. You're a mighty brave lady. Want some coffee?"

"Yeah, thanks." Sandy helped her into the van and poured her a cup.

"Right now I don't feel so brave. Just awfully tired."

"Hey, no kidding. They figure you had to go twenty miles across some pretty rough country, and at night. Anybody would be tired. Just lay back and relax. The sheriff should be along pretty soon."

Kathy dropped into a dreamlike trance. She was faintly aware that there were voices and motion around her, but none of it mattered. Every muscle in her whole body was tired, but it didn't matter. She felt great as long as she didn't have to move. She felt as though she was the first leg of the mile relay. She'd handed off the baton and now it was up to somebody else. Her part was done. She was faintly aware of motion again, and flashing lights, then she totally passed out.

"Sheriff Roybal, what can you tell us about the alleged kidnappers?" Most of the reporters scribbled furiously while the two with the video camera asked the questions.

"Well, they're both local guys. We're not giving out their names 'til we find out if there's other people involved."

"So you think there's others involved?"

"No, I don't think that. I just don't know."

"Are they in custody?"

"One of them is in custody, he turned himself in last night. The other one, we know where he's at. We'll have him in custody in a day or two."

"You say, 'in a day or two', does that mean..."

"That's all the information I have right now."

"Dr. Jackson, you've identified a man in custody as one of your alleged kidnappers, is that right?"

"That's correct."

"What kind of work were you engaged in, sir?"

"We were doing field studies for commercially usable oil shale in the area."

"When you say 'we', sir, with whom were you working at the time?"

"Mr. Tom Smith and Miss Kathy Kendall."

"I understand that Miss Kendall managed to escape from captivity and this distracted the alleged kidnappers to the extent that you and Mr. Smith were able to escape as well."

"That's true. Miss Kendall's actions made it possible for all of us to return to safety."

"Is there any other comment you'd like to make, Dr. Jackson?"

"Yes, I'd like to express my appreciation to the Hidalgo County Sheriff's Office and the group of volunteers whose actions helped us to reach safety. And special thanks to my colleague, Miss Kathy Kendall for her bravery."

"Thank you, Dr. Jackson. You have just heard from Howard Jackson, a petroleum geologist, who, while prospecting for oil shale, along with Tom Smith and Kathy Kendall, was abducted and held in captivity for six hours by two armed men. Miss Kendall, a former high school track star, managed to escape and covered twenty miles on foot, over very rough terrain, to obtain help for her two co-workers. From Hidalgo County New Mexico, this is Russ Russton for ABC News."

Jim Taylor sat up on the couch and reached for the phone. He pushed eleven digits.

"Information, what city please?"

"Marshall."

"May I help you?"

"A Kendall, K-E-N-D-A-L-L-, on Comfrey Cove." Jim memorized the number and punched again.

"Hello."

"Mrs. Kendall? This is Jim Taylor."

"Hello, Jim. I guess you just watched the news."

"Yes, I did. Your daughter's terrific, isn't she? Have you spoken with her yet?"

"No, I just heard it on the news myself."

"Well, I'm sure she'll be calling soon. Give her my best and ask her to call me, will you?"

"I sure will, Jim, as soon as I hear from her. Thank you for calling."

"I'll talk to you later. Goodbye."

The tears welled up in Ann's eyes. That wild, wonderful red-headed girl. What will she be up to next?

Kathy was sitting at a table in the sheriff's office. It was about ten PM, eight hours after she first saw Sandy's car on the highway. She was surrounded by law officers, two reporters, one of whom was a sixteen year old girl, and Tom and Jack. She was trying to eat a quarter-pounder and talk to Jim Taylor on the phone at the same time.

"... just promise me one thing, Jim- no, just one thing. Next chance we get, we're going camping. Yes, I'll pick the place. Leave it to me. No, I'm not kidding. Well you better, dammit! Yes I do. Ok, well listen, I've got a whole mess of people to talk to, so I'll call you back later. Yeah... you too. Ok, bye."

The sixteen year old started, "Well how does it feel to be known all over as a big hero?"

"Oh, god, no. I'm no... I only did what anybody else would do under the circumstances. Look, I thought I'd slip out, make it to the highway, get help and go back. But see, these guys really deserve the credit. They made sure I was safe..." Her eyes teared up. "The whole time I thought, if I can make it back in time..." She began sobbing. "But they were ok all along."

Tom grabbed her by the shoulders. "That's enough of that talk, young lady. How can you say that? Neither of us could have made it out the way you did. Getting away clean was what sent the big guy off into the bushes without taking the keys out of the ignition. Jack and I wouldn't be here now if it wasn't for you. You saved my life, dammit."

Kathy had one arm around Jack, the other around Tom. Her face was beet red. Her face was wet with tears. "You guys are the best friends anyone ever had."

The young reporter was scribbling away madly. Jack spoke, "Why hell yes, I'd do anything for you right now."

"You would? I think I could eat another hamburger."

JEFFERSON HERALD, Jefferson, Todd County, Nebraska. October sixth 1980.

THE MIDDLE OF NOWHERE

Headline: CANTERING KATE WINS AGAIN! Two gunmen in rural New Mexico, who decided to kidnap a team of geologists, were unaware that the female member of the party was former Central High track star Kathleen 'Cantering Kate' Kendall; district record holder of the women's mile and mile relay. Kendall slipped through a window, under the cover of darkness and made her way cross country in excess of twenty miles, to elude her captors and bring help to her colleagues. Her effort so startled the would-be kidnappers that all three members of the group succeeded in escaping the gunmen unharmed. This reporter spoke with Miss Kendall by phone early this morning. She said, 'Oh, it was nothing that anyone wouldn't have done; but I did it for a special reason. There's someone else who would have done it for me.' Kathy, daughter of Mrs. Ann Kendall of Marshall, will be in Jefferson this weekend (she promised) for a few hours- that is if she isn't too embarrassed."

Ann smiled. "Good ol' Bob. Life would get dull."

Sandy stayed around for a few hours and talked to some TV news people, then headed back to the van. He had been on the road a long time and he really felt an urge to stay in one place for a while and let his nerves unravel. Between himself and Barbara, they had made the retail business make money once again; although it had gone through a major transformation in the process. It was still the 'Orient Express', but the type of merchandise, and the way it was displayed, were significantly different. They now had Native American arts and crafts, and imports from many parts of the world, instead of concentrating on oriental goods. He didn't spend too much time wondering about whether or not Jake would have approved of the changes they had made.

He thought about Jake a good deal, but his concern centered mainly around where Jake was, and if he was still alive. He had notified the American Embassy in every country where there might be the remotest chance that Jake was there. He or Barbara had chased down every possible thread of hope there might be that he was being held somewhere.

From the time Jake had left, back in April, Sandy had made the decisions as they came. He had mainly taken the approach that profit margin took precedence over every other consideration.

There had been a few windfalls that had effected major changes in their type of business. With the help of Bob and Louise, he had started doing business with Win Davis in No Name. Win had made, first, branding irons, and then kitchen hardware for Sandy. It had started out to be retail and later expanded to the point that they were selling Win's stuff to other dealers.

Even before that, Sandy had pulled off an incredible deal for some Native American jewelry. At an estate sale, he had bought a huge private collection with a bid of a hundred and fifty-five dollars. When he took the jewelry to have it appraised, he found it was old 'pawn' jewelry that, if sold retail, would be worth twenty thousand. Wherever the trade winds had blown him, he planted seeds—and mainly roses had come up. But none of it had he been able to relish. It seemed to have no purpose. It was only money. For one thing, most of the progress he had made had been out on the road, and all the miles had worn into his mind like cracks in concrete pavement. But even so, he hadn't felt like sitting still either. He could almost feel at ease as long as he was moving. As long as his mind stayed occupied, he didn't have to brood. He was pleased with their new store. It looked nice, inside and out. The location was great. It was in an area of specialty shops with plenty of parking. But he couldn't stand to be there very long.

Sometimes he thought about Louise. It was a bright spot in a mostly shadowy year. She had a quality about her he couldn't quite define. She seemed to be a part of the land on which she lived. But a girl like her could never get used to the style of life he knew. He was pure business, and his type of business depended on urban life.

He headed east out of Arroyo Alto toward I-25. Once on the interstate, he let the engine wind up longer as he climbed a long, sloping ridge on his way up the Sangre de Christo range. It was getting on towards evening. The sky felt like a warm blanket covering the bare shoulders of the earth from the deep black of space. Eventually he shifted back into third gear and continued his long climb up to the pass. He needed to call Barbara. He needed to talk to Louise. He could call her after six and talk for a while. It was always pleasant- something to smile about. He needed to talk to Win Davis, too. Before he took anymore orders for wrought iron, he needed to find out how much Win was capable of producing.

The van was fairly loaded down. He had invested in some Chimayo rugs. They were produced by some horizontal-loom weavers in Northern New Mexico. The rugs had added about three hundred pounds to his load. He figured to be able to turn them over at a good profit when he got back to Virginia. Something about the Chimayo weavers kept nagging at his mind. They were hand weavers, native to their area. They were good crafts people, but they were also very businesslike. They had a unique product, and if the world wasn't exactly beating a path to their door, at least handcraft traders had been for quite some time. And it was a well-worn path indeed. He stopped when he got to Springer. He called Barbara's home and gave the operator his credit card number. "Hello."

"Hi, Barb, how're things going?"

143

"Fine. How are you?"

"I'm ok. I'm on my way back."

"Louise wants you to call her right away."

"Yeah, I'll call her. I need to give you a rundown…"

"She said it was urgent."

"Is she all right?"

"Yes, I think so. She didn't want to try to explain it. She wanted to talk to you first."

"I guess I'll call her now, and call you back later."

"I think you should. We can talk later."

"Ok, thanks for the message." Sandy hung up. He couldn't imagine what Louise might want. He wasn't in the mood to talk about future plans. He didn't know how things would be in the future. As long as he didn't know about Jake, he couldn't be making any plans. He sat there in the phone booth for several minutes, trying to settle his mind down so he could call. Finally, he picked up the phone and dialed. The operator came on and he gave her his credit card number. The phone rang.

"Hello."

"Louise?"

"Sandy! Thank God it's you! Listen, something happened…" Her voice was shaky.

"Just take it easy, Louise, it's all right."

"I know it sounds crazy, but just hear me out for a few minutes. Ok?"

"Ok, ok, just relax."

"I'm trying. Listen, there's a little boy here- the son of a friend of mine. He's deaf, but he can read lips. She called me."

"Who called you?"

"My friend. Just wait a second. She said they were watching the news on TV, and this British reporter was inside this prison in Iran. Well, Tommie- that's the little boy, he starts pointing at someone in the background. And he told Opal, his mother, 'that man is saying Sand Rose, Sand Rose.' So she remembered me saying your name, so she called me. She said, 'Wasn't your friend's name Sandy

144

Rose?' What do you think?"

"I don't know what to think. I need to see for myself, I guess. But Jake wouldn't have gone to Iran in a million years. When did this happen?"

"It was on the six o'clock news on CBS. Maybe they'll air it again at nine or ten, or whenever the late news is on. Do you think there's a chance?"

"Anything's possible. But I'm not getting my hopes up too high. What time is it there?"

"Ten after seven. But wait, Sandy, there's more."

"What?"

"Bob's getting married. My brother's getting married. You remember Wanda? She's coming to live here."

"Wait a second- too much information. Ok, Bob's getting married- what's that got to do…?

"It doesn't, it doesn't. We'll talk about it later."

Sandy took a few breaths. "Listen, I'll watch the late news and see what happens. I'll call back right after that, ok?"

"Yes. Just one more thing."

"Yeah?"

"I miss you!"

"I understand. I'll call back as soon as I can. Bye now." Sandy hung up. He was feeling shaky. There were too many maybes. He would wait to call Barbara later.

He felt like he needed a drink. There was a small bar across the highway. When he went in, they were speaking Spanish. The conversation stopped when they saw him. The bartender asked, "What can I get you, partner?"

"Scotch and water. Got anything to eat?"

"Chili and sandwiches."

"Chili sounds good. Does the TV work?"

"Yeah, we don't usually turn it on unless there's a game."

Sandy explained about what Louise had told him. It wasn't long before everybody in the place- which amounted to two men in their sixties, and one in his forties, besides the bartender, were eager to find out if the mysterious news cast held the key to finding his brother's whereabouts. The news would be on at nine. The Bartender's name was Noe. The two older men were Jose and Carlos The younger man was Rolando.

Noe didn't speak too much English, but when they told him about it, he grinned and gave Sandy the thumbs-up sign. It felt good to be around kindred spirits. Big city people were never that way. He bought a round of drinks, and then they, one by one, started buying drinks for him. The chili was good and the liquor made him feel more relaxed. He decided he should take it slow, it wouldn't do to not be able to see straight when the news came on. At eight-thirty Noe turned on the set but left the sound turned down. The minutes crept by. Sandy realized he was breathing hard in his nervousness. He concentrated on breathing slowly just to get in control again.

When a commercial break began, the bartender turned up the sound. A few minutes later a newsman was saying, "...and a BBC correspondent will be taking us inside a prison in Teheran where it has been rumored that some of the fifty-five American hostages are being held." The room became very quiet. All eyes were glued to the TV screen. Sandy got up and stood at the end of the bar so he was only five feet from the set. A few minutes later they heard, "... not certain where the fifty-five Americans are being held, but prison officials said..." The BBC reporter was holding a microphone. All around him were vertical bars with faces of dozens of men looking out. Sandy groaned. His heart was pounding. He was frozen in place- there were so many faces. There wasn't enough time to tell. Rolando pointed to the screen.

"There! Hey man, right there!"

Sandy jumped. "Where?"

"Lower right! Right there!"

A face was moving back and forth. The mouth was moving. The face was dark and bearded, and out of focus, but the mouth was unmistakable. It was Jake. "God, it's him!" Sandy slapped both hands on the top of the bar. He nearly fell over backwards. Tears welled up in his eyes. Jose and Carlos grabbed his arms and helped him to a chair. He was crying uncontrollably. They stood around him, patting him on the back and offering their support. It was several minutes before he was able to talk.

Jose was saying, "It's ok, man, you found your brother. Let it all out. That's the best way." The bartender put a fresh drink in front of him. He took a swallow and then wiped his eyes with his napkin.

Noe said, "Just sit here as long as you want. It's ok."

"Thanks, you guys, thanks to all of you."

"That's ok, Pal." said Carlos. "We know how you feel."

"Man, I would call President Carter," said Rolando.

"If you need any help, like a witness or something... just let us know." said Noe.

Sandy was just beginning to regain his composure when he called Barbara.

"Hello."

"Hello," Barb, "get in touch with the state department..."

"What happened?" Sandy broke into tears again.

"It's Jake? Sandy? Is he all right?"

"Oh... yeah... wait a second." When he regained his composure, he began again. Now Barbara was feeling shaky. Sandy finally got the story across. She told him she would get the political forces in motion.

Sandy said, "I've got to call Louise. I'd better let you go."

"Ok, Sandy. Oh, I'm so happy. Are you all right?"

"Yeah, I've got some friends helping me. I'll get back with you. Bye." He hung up. Then he called the Gages.

"Sandy?"

"Yeah, it's me."

"Was it...?"

"Yeah, it's him. It's Jake."

"My god! Oh, Sandy, I'm so happy for you! How did he get there? What are you going to do...?"

"Don't know yet. Barb's calling the State Department. We'll get him out somehow. He wouldn't have gone there on purpose. It's got to be a mix-up."

"So, are you going home now or what?"

"Well...I thought maybe I'd stop in and see you guys. If it's all right."

"Oh, sure! Hey, great! We'd love it."

"Well, then… guess I'll see you when I get there."

"All right! Well, drive careful! Oh, I'm so glad, Sandy."

"See you later."

"Ok, bye."

By the time Sandy had made his farewells at the bar, it was after 10 pm. It was slow going until he topped Raton Pass, but once he got on the downhill side, he made better time. It was just about midnight as he neared Pueblo, Colorado, but he didn't feel like sleeping. The day's events were still occupying his mind. There were a lot of questions that he kept trying to work through by logic- but, in this case, logic really didn't work. He wished he had someone to talk to, just to occupy his mind. It was difficult to overcome the tendency to mash down on the accelerator. He had already been through his box of tapes too many times on this trip. He turned on the radio and searched for a station. First he came to a call-in show. Then he came to a religious station. The next station he reached was playing vintage country swing. He left it there. For some reason, at the time you need most for your radio to keep you awake, it becomes the most boring.

At a truck stop close to Denver, he drank a cup of coffee and ate a sweet roll. When he's paid his check, he went in the gift shop and looked around. Almost everything there had something to proclaim. What could he get for a ten-year-old kid who had found his only brother? He needed something that proclaimed,

"Tommy Worth- International Hero!"

He picked out a folding Buck knife from the display on the counter.

"You're not going to give this to somebody, are you?" said the lady at the counter.

"Yep. Best friend I've got and I don't even know him."

"Well, put a penny in the box with it so it won't cut your friendship."

"Oh, yeah?"

"It's what they say."

Sandy smiled and put the knife in his pocket. He stopped at the pumps and filled the tank, then got back on the interstate. He took the exit onto 76 and headed east. As he approached Ft. Morgan, the sun was creeping up on the horizon. He put on his sunglasses and stuck a road map up against the wind shield to block the direct sunlight.

76 merged with 80 right at the state border. When he saw the sign that read "Welcome to Nebraska" he let out a yelp. It was 7:30 when he came to the "No Name" exit. His heart was pounding as he headed up the Gage's road. As he drove into the yard, smoke was rising from the chimney. He hadn't yet shut off the engine when the kitchen door flew open. Louise bounded out of the door at a dead run. She tackled Sandy ten feet from the van. Tears were streaming down her face.

"Oh, my god, Sandy, how did you get here so fast?"

"Had to fly low, under the radar."

"God, what can I say?"

"Just say welcome home, ok?"

"Welcome home."

Sandy and Louise entered the house arm in arm. Bob and Wanda were sitting together on the sofa. They both had wide grins. Wanda had a firm grip on Bob's wrist with her right hand. She had what she'd always wanted- a man to share her life, and she couldn't quite get used to the fact that he wasn't going away.

After the introductions, Bob said, "Well, Sandy, we've heard all about Jake. Tell us about your adventure right before that."

"It was about an amazing woman named Kathy Kendall. She's a geologist for an oil exploration business. She and her two colleagues were abducted by a couple of gun-toting, misguided individuals who thought they were prospecting for gemstones. It happened when someone was eavesdropping on a conversation and came to a false conclusion. To make a long story short, Kathy escaped and ran for help. She had been a track star from back when she was a teenager. She lives in Denver, and, we found out later, she just happens to be the girlfriend of Wanda's brother."

"Oh, yay," said Wanda. "Jim had been telling me about this tall redheaded woman he was so fond of. As far as I'm concerned, if she winds up being my sister-in-law, I'll be overjoyed. Anybody who would do what she did is a credit to the whole female gender."

Louise said: "Sandy, you must be pretty tired by now, or is that an understatement?"

"Yes, I would agree- whole-heartedly. But before I head in that direction I want to hear about your own sister-in-law." Sandy related.

"By all means. Most importantly, my brother loves her. And she wants to make her home here on this ranch. But I think I'd prefer to have her tell you about herself."

"My name is Wanda Taylor. I'm thirty-five years old. I became an LPN ten years ago. Most recently I've been working with elderly people in a residential care home. I love horses. I tried to be a barrel racer. Had a certain amount of success. Then I met Bob, and he told me he had a sister named Louise. She happens to be the best barrel rider that ever lived. I can hardly believe what's happened lately. Bob and Louise own and operate this ranch, here in Nebraska. I met Bob, and he asked me if I wanted to marry him and come live on this ranch. And the rest, as they say, is history."

"Well," said Sandy, "You guys know about Jake, but there's just a lot of things I need to tell you about myself and what's happening with me. But right at the moment I need to get in a horizontal position before I fall down on the floor."

They were all nodding their heads since they all understood Sandy's dilemma.

Louise said, "Why don't you lay down on the sofa and relax. Have you had anything to eat lately?"

"Actually I haven't, but don't bother with that right now. Just let me catch up on my sleep and I'll be ready to share a meal with you guys whenever I come back to life." The sofa was abandoned by Wanda and Bob and Sandy took their place.

Sandy didn't wake until 10:00 AM. They were enjoying waffles and bacon when the phone rang. Louise answered it. It was for Sandy.

"Sandy Rose."

"Hi, Sandy, it's Barbara. I told State about your identification of Jake in the BBC news broadcast. I've got a number for you to call. Ask to speak with a Robin Marquardt. She'll be handling the case going forward. Apparently you'll need to be coming back here. Are you going to be able to do that?"

"Oh, sure. Let me have the number- I'll get on it right away."

"Well, guys. Is it ok if I call the state department? They want to talk to me personally. I'll use my credit card."

"Ok with me," said Bob. "Do you need some privacy?"

"Nah, I've got nothing to hide, I'm happy to say."

When Sandy had Ms. Marquardt on the phone, she started by verifying that he was Sanford L. Rose nee Rosenblum. They decided to address each other as 'Sandy' and 'Robin'.

She said, "Now, you're at least 90 percent positive that the man you saw on the newscast was your brother, Jacob?"

"Oh, I'd say 99.9 percent positive."

"So, he had a USA passport- and why would he be abroad, was it business?"

"Yes, we're in the oriental import-gift shop business. He was just purchasing merchandise for our store."

"I see. Then might he have been in Iran for that reason?"

"We have traded Persian rugs in the past. But with the current situation in that part of the world, which he was well aware of, I'd find it hard to believe he would have gone there intentionally."

"I see. Well, even with the present confrontation, they would have no valid reason to detain an American citizen who was simply engaged in a legitimate business."

"I see your point, but I'm certain my brother wouldn't knowingly have gone there."

"All right, we'll just assume that to be the case. Now, what are your plans for the immediate future?"

"Within the next day or two, I'll be returning to the DC area. That's where my gift shop, Orient Express, is located. I'll contact you when I arrive."

"All right, Sandy. We're just getting started in this process. Several department employees will be contacted- we'll contact your brother as quick as we can. Please notify us as soon as you arrive, and we'll continue our discussion. Have a safe trip."

"Thank you, Robin. I'll be seeing you very soon. Goodbye." Sandy hung up the phone.

"Well, folks, The U.S. Department of State is now in charge of getting my brother back home again. I feel a lot better about it, but I'll feel even better about it when I get to talk to him."

Louise said, "Wow, I know you've been bothered about this for a long time. At least now you can sleep easier, knowing there's something being done."

"And let me say," said Bob, "If Louise wants to take this opportunity to go see Sandy's place, it's ok with me. Wanda and I can take care of things for the time being."

"And, while we're on the subject," said Wanda, "I'm positive there are some young people around northern Colorado who would be tickled pink to come out here and spend a week or two- take a break from school or day-labor."

"What do you think, Sandy?" Louise enthused.

"Oh, hey," Sandy replied, "I can damn sure use some company- it's been very lonely out there on the road the last few months."

They had to drive the van to Virginia because it was almost fully loaded with merchandise for the Orient Express. Louise had to figure out what she wanted to take with her. She asked Sandy what kind of clothes she needed to take.

"My dear, all I can tell you, is what you don't need."

"And what does that include?"

"Oh, just the things you would need in cold weather. It won't be cold."

"No, it won't be cold, but what do I need to wear?"

"Pretty much whatever you wear all the time."

"But I wear jeans and button-up shirts most of the time."

"Women on the East Coast wear jeans too. They'll be wearing such a wide variety of clothes, you won't ever be out of place. You're a western girl, you may as well dress like one. Men and women will just think, there's a 'western girl.' We walk on the pavement a lot, so you might want to have sneakers. If you get into a situation where you want to wear something you don't have, then I'll buy it for you. Barbara, and other women, will be around to give you wardrobe advice."

"You're so damned agreeable, Sandy. But I know I can trust you."

152

Louise had the feeling that she could take anything that struck her fancy. It was nice to have a partner that was so accommodating.

"What else besides clothing do I need," she asked Sandy.

"If you've got some cassette tapes you like, bring them along. I've been listening to the same ones the last six months, and I'm pretty bored with them."

Sandy was looking at the dipstick in his van when Bob walked over. Sandy said, "I guess I don't need an oil change, but maybe I need a tune-up."

"I'll show you how to check if you need a tune-up. Let me loosen the ignition wires on this engine, then you can start it up." Bob loosened the wires to the distributor cap, then he told Sandy to start the engine. One by one he disconnected the wires as he listened to the engine. There was a noticeable change each time a wire was removed. "Your engine is running on all six cylinders." Bob moved the carburetor linkage to rev up the engine, "It sounds good and you've got good power. Now, all you need to do is pull out each spark-plug and look at the electrodes. If they're brown, that's good. Look at the gaps and see if they're within range. Use this feeler gauge to check the gaps."

"That's all I need to do?" asked Sandy.

"That's all you need to do to check it. If something isn't right you have to fix it."

"Wow, thanks Bob. How did you learn all this?"

"When you grow up in the country you learn a lot of things that city kids don't need to know."

When Louise and Sandy had the van loaded, they said their farewells to Bob and Wanda and headed for I-80. They would be traveling on interstates until they reached Virginia. Sandy felt like he had to get there as soon as he could. Having someone to help with driving was a thing he felt thankful for. He had Robin's phone number if he felt a need to check in. He asked Louise, "How do you feel about your new sister-in-law?"

"She loves my brother- that's one good thing. But on another level, she loves horses and she loves the situation she's in, so I couldn't feel better about her."

Sandy said, "I'm so happy to have you with me, I can't tell you how much."

153

"I think I understand. Right now, there's no other place I'd rather be."

"As we move eastward, you're going to see a big increase in population. I think you know that, but seeing it with your own eyes might be somewhat daunting."

Louise nodded her head. "As long as I'm with you, I'll be able to handle it. We'll be in McClean, Virginia, right?"

"That's right," Sandy replied. "The address of the new shop is in Arlington, Virginia. But you won't see any sign that you're going from one urban center to another."

THE MIDDLE OF NOWHERE

THE REST OF THE STORY

Louise and Sandy reached Arlington at 3:00 in the afternoon. Barbara was expecting them. She had called a temp agency for two workers to help unload the van. They were twenty-somethings and seemed enthusiastic about helping in a retail business. Barbara showed them the area where they wanted the bulk of the merchandise to be unloaded. When they got the process started, Sandy went to the phone to call Robin Marquardt.

"Sandy Rose here. What do we have going, so far?"

"Hi, Sandy, we should be hearing from the department soon. You'll be pleased to know that your brother is out of foreign custody and is on his way to a secure station where we'll be able to speak to him, very soon."

"Ah, thank God! That's just what I wanted to hear. So, is he in Europe now?"

"I don't know if it's Europe, in any case it's a NATO country. After they've done some debriefing, he'll be able to call me. Can you come by my office tomorrow?"

"Oh, sure. Can I bring my significant other along?"

"That would be fine. So, you're no longer single?"

"I'm happy to say, yes."

"You have the address?"

"Yes, I do. What time?"

"Make it 10:00, they should be ready by then."

They made it to the State Department building at 9:45. Robin invited them in. "Sandy, we finally meet."

Sandy introduced her to Louise and they all sat down. "We're waiting for the call, it shouldn't take very long." In eight minutes the phone rang. "Marquardt."

"Hi, Robin, Doug Pendleton here. I'm calling from an Air Force facility in Turkey. I have Jacob Rose with me. I understand you have a relative there with you who'd like to speak with him."

"Yes, it's his brother." She handed the phone to Sandy.

"Sandy, is that you?"

Sandy closed his eyes, "Yeah, Jake, it's me. Are you ok?"

"Oh, I could be better, but I'm ok, I'm fine. How are you?"

Sandy realized he was holding his breath, then tried to relax. "I'm fine. I'm just... so relieved that you're alive."

"Yeah, yeah, me too. Listen, I'll be here for a couple of days. Then they'll send me home. I'll fly into Dulles. I'll let you know before then. Anything else?"

"Uh, just one thing. I'm getting married soon. After you get back. Here, I'll give you back to Robin. Take care."

Louise threw her arms around Sandy. They were both crying.

When they picked up Jake at the airport, all he had was carry-on luggage. He looked like a man who hadn't had any sleep for a long time. He and Sandy embraced for a long time. For several seconds they both tried to speak, but each one stopped to let the other start. Finally, Louise said. "Ok, Jake, you start."

Jake said, "Let's go to the store. We can talk on the way."

"If you don't have any luggage, let's go to the car," said Sandy. "It's a long walk, are you ok walking?"

"Oh, I'd love to walk. I haven't walked in god knows how long."

When they got to the van, Louise said, "I'd drive but I'm new here."

"That's ok, I'll drive," said Sandy. When they were out on the street Jake started talking.

"In case you're wondering, I do not know what they arrested me for, or why they held me. Can I just tell you what went on?"

"Go ahead," said Sandy. "Just assume I don't know anything, which is, basically, true."

"Ok, there's a guy named James Brennan, who I met in Hong Kong. He's an Englishman. He's a dealer in arts and crafts work, not that different to what we do. We had a long talk. I told him we were interested in Pakistan and Afghanistan. You know, of course, what happened in Afghanistan." Sandy nodded. "But we were there, for a brief period of time. James has lots of contacts in India, Sri Lanka, Pakistan and Malaysia. And there are dealers in all these places, so you don't have to go very far to get your hands on a lot of neat stuff."

156

"James had the use of this Toyota minivan. Belonged to some Pakistani people. We were on our way into Afghanistan just having a good old time. We ran into some people who made embroidered hats and vests and we bought, maybe, $200 worth of stuff. Then we got word about the Russians invading. So immediately we thought, let's go back to Pakistan. So we're driving back south, along the same road we came in on. It was along the border with Iran, but the border was at least thirty miles away. Man, we were in the middle of nowhere. Now if you're coming to a border, there's got to be a sign to let you know that. So, we're just driving south on the same road to Pakistan we came in on. Well, we look up ahead, and we see these soldiers in the road. They stop us and want to see our papers. I don't know what language they spoke, apparently Farsi, but the communication was just the pits. So James had a UK passport, I had a US passport, so they took me, at gunpoint, into custody. That's the last I saw of James. They let him go. He's got a lot of my stuff, but I'm sure I can find him."

Sandy said, "Did they think you were a spy, or what?"

"I don't know. I guess they tried to swap the hostages for the Shah. Maybe they thought one more American would help their case. But I've been listening to these Embassy people for quite some time. They've been saying that, regardless of where I was, arresting me was a violation of international law. And, as far as that goes, President Carter had frozen Iran's assets in our banks and they would forfeit tons of money if they didn't cooperate. Besides that, if any harm came to any of the US citizens, it was an act of war."

Sandy added, "Yeah, Reagan won the election, but he was not the president at the time this all took place."

Jake said, "Iran had already kicked out the Shah once before, in the Nixon administration, and our country put him back in power again. Reagan said he wouldn't have let the Shah be overthrown. That's the type of people we have running this country."

When they arrived back at the store, Barbara gave Jake a big hug. She shed a few tears as Jake continued to relate his adventures in the Far East. Barbara had hired another clerk to help with running the store. Her name was Violet and she was Puerto Rican.

Eventually, Jake and Sandy opened a store in Ogallala, Nebraska. It was a retail/wholesale outlet. They carried a lot of American made crafts. It was close to the Gage ranch. Louise loved being close to her brother, and Sandy had developed an attachment to the Sand Hills. One of the people they dealt with was a leather craftsman, Wes George, who had sold the bay gelding, Rattler, to the Walker family so many years ago.

THE END